OFF THE WALL 2

AN URBAN ROMANCE SERIES

TY RINGO

OFF THE WALL 2 NOTE

To my readers:

Off the Wall 2 is back with the same crew from the first volume, a little older and maybe a little wiser. As they deal with the issues that come their way, can they hold it together as their worlds continuously change around them?

Please keep in mind that though this book is fiction, it is still based on real-life scenarios and situations. With that in mind, understand that just because it may not seem realistic to you, does not mean it is not realistic to others, but is purely coincidental and not meant to emulate anyone's reality specifically.

Off the Wall 2 may be triggering to some, as it contains violence, sexual scenes, and adult language. If any of the themes mentioned before cause any type of trauma to arise, I ask that you NOT continue with this read.

This story is the second of three novels that revolve around these characters through different stages of their lives.

I hope you enjoy reading as much as I enjoyed writing.

♥♥♥

TABLE OF CONTENTS

PART III

"It's like I was playing some kind of game, but the rules
don't make any sense to me. They're being made up by all
the wrong people."
-The Graduate

1

———

KIARA

FOUR YEARS LATER...

"**M**ercy, stop playing with me and come on," Kiara told the little girl who had her face scrunched up with her lips pouted.

"But Mommy...I don't wanna go. It's boring," Mercy pouted to her mother who couldn't care less what her daughter was saying.

Kiara looked at her three-year-old toddler that would be four in a few short months and released a deep sigh. Mercy had too much of her father in her and was stubborn to the point of madness. She was also smart for her age and because of the great schooling she had been getting since she started walking, could speak complete sentences well and was already learning the alphabet and numbers in English and Spanish.

She honestly didn't disagree with her daughter, but knew they had to go. Though Kiara had a less than pleasing relationship with her father, Rodrick Atkins, he made sure to be a part of his granddaughter's life.

Kiara didn't know how to feel about it, but her mother told her to let the relationship happen and if he messed up, then she could cut it. She reluctantly agreed and he and his wife had been present, especially his wife. Lisa and Mercy spent a lot of time together and Kiara preferred their bond to her father's and Mercy's.

"Ci-Ci, do this for Mommy, okay? Maybe afterwards, Grandma and Auntie Renee can take you to get your nails done or something." At the mention of getting pampered, Mercy's hazel eyes lit up and she hurriedly got her Doc McStuffins backpack and ran to the front door to leave. Kiara just shook her head at her spoiled little one and grabbed her keys so they could take the drive to her father's house.

While Mercy's attention was on her tablet watching cartoons, Kiara's eyes found her left hand and another deep sigh passed her lips. She missed her husband horribly. It had been four years since his incarceration and her world turned upside down.

Chi had been charged with possession of a controlled substance and intent to distribute. If he hadn't been holding the cocaine in his hands when the police busted down the trap house's door, he possibly could have gotten the charges dropped or at least reduced to probation, but he'd been caught red handed. Luckily, he only had a couple of bricks and they hadn't been able to find more. It didn't matter though because Chi had to serve seven to ten years, but his lawyers still worked overtime to get him out sooner.

Kiara fell into a deep depression after finding out he had been arrested. Her mother, sister-in-law, and best friend let her mope around for a little while but made her put her big girl panties on soon after. After crying her eyes out during their first visit, Kiara let Chi know about the baby and talked about their future and how things would go.

Somehow, it wasn't as difficult a time as she thought it

would be. It probably had something to do with how much weight the Jackson name carried because Chi made sure to call, text, and FaceTime her constantly with a phone he'd gotten on the inside. She was also able to see him pretty often as well so even though he wasn't physically there every step of the way, he still made sure to step up.

He also loved his daughter and she loved him, too. She was too young to understand what was going on so she and her family always told Mercy he was away for work, but they made sure she spoke and saw him often through FaceTime. She was definitely a daddy's girl.

"Mommy?" Mercy called out from the backseat. She kept flipping her beaded braids in and out of her face and Kiara knew she'd have to pin them so she would leave them alone.

"Yes, Ci-Ci?"

"Is Uncle Eric gonna be there? Oooo or Uncle Reggie?" Mercy asked excitedly.

"I haven't talked to Eric today, baby, but Uncle Reggie said he was stopping by," Kiara said and looked in her rear view mirror to see Mercy grinning and tuning back into her show.

Eric was Kiara's older brother by two years through her dad and the only sibling she got along with. Her whore of a father had five children that everyone knew about: three boys with his wife Lisa, and two outside of his marriage, Eric and Kiara. She wouldn't say she and Eric were black sheeps of the family, but they definitely weren't the most loved, but that was okay because they were close and had a great family outside of their father's family unit. That great family included her father's younger brother, Reggie.

Reggie was an amazing uncle to her and Mercy absolutely adored him. He'd gone into business with his brother and they owned several throughout Chicago, but they were polar opposites. Where Rodrick was arrogant and sometimes self serving, Reggie was humble and one of the most selfless people Kiara knew. She was amazingly close to him and considered him to be the father figure she always wanted.

Pulling up to her father's house she turned off her car and turned around to face her daughter. She looked her over and smiled. She looked just like a young Moriah except she had Kiara's java brown skin tone and wavy long hair that was currently braided into two ponytails with beaded braids hanging down in the front. Before they could even knock on the front door, Rodrick's wife, Lisa, opened it and smiled down at Mercy.

"Hi, Grandma Lisa," Mercy spoke before running past her and into the house. Lisa looked at Kiara and gave a small smile before turning around and going back to the kitchen. Kiara turned to close the door. She counted to ten and walked further into the house to see her three oldest brothers and two of their women sitting in the living room with their father.

"Ah, KiKi, there you are. Didn't know if we'd see your face today or if you had to take a trip," her oldest brother RJ's wife said. Kam always told Kiara that she was just jealous because even though she'd had plastic surgery to enhance every single asset she had, Kiara still looked much better.

"No, I figured I'd save the trip and take it with you so we can visit him and *both* your brothers all at once," Kiara stated before canting her head with a raised eyebrow. She could tell Ahsia wasn't expecting her response because her face fell before it tightened and she turned away from Kiara's stare.

Another reason why Kiara hated coming over was

because she felt that they looked down on her for being involved with a Jackson "thug." The fact that he'd gone to prison didn't help matters.

It was crazy though, seeing that Ahsia came from the hood and had two brothers that were both in maximum security prisons and would be there for years to come, but because she'd married into the Atkins family, she and everyone else had forgotten where she came from and her own family issues.

Kiara looked at them all before scoffing and headed to the kitchen where Mercy and Lisa were. Kiara actually loved her stepmother. She was a sweet woman who came from old money and was taught that she had to cater to her husband, but she always treated Kiara fairly and with much more love than her father could muster up for her.

The only problem that she had with Lisa was that she lacked a backbone when it came to her husband and sons. Clearly her husband couldn't keep his dick in his pants and her sons didn't treat her with the respect she deserved, but she never said anything and Kiara could never get with that. She learned long ago though that it was just who she was as a person and the fact that they took advantage of that saddened and angered her.

"What are you two doing in here?" she smiled softly at them. Lisa was helping Mercy cut out cookies so they could bake.

"Look, Mommy. Cookies!" Mercy exclaimed excitedly with her deep dimples making an appearance.

"I see. That looks great, mama," Kiara said before she sat at the kitchen table watching them.

"So Lisa, how are you?"

"Oh, I can't complain, dear. Just trying to make it one day at a time," Lisa answered before smiling at Kiara.

Before she could respond, Rodrick walked into the kitchen and kissed the top of Mercy's head and told them he was leaving. Kiara did nothing but roll her eyes.

"But Rod, dinner is almost done. You don't want to wait a few minutes?" Lisa asked her husband sweetly, but Kiara could tell that she was upset. She also knew Lisa would never speak on it.

"Well, put it up for later, Lisa. Me and the boys are leaving but the girls are staying here and I think Reggie is stopping by too so it'll get eaten one way or another. I'll be back later tonight so don't wait up," Rodrick told her without even looking back.

Lisa stood still for a few moments before she caught Kiara's eye and gave her a tight smile. She didn't want to, but Kiara returned it. She mentally added yet another reason to her list as to why she disliked the man that helped make her.

After sitting down for an awkward dinner, Ahsia and Kiara's other brother Rodney's girlfriend left for their own homes. Kiara stayed to help clean up. As she was washing the countertop down, she heard the front door open and heard her daughter squeal and knew her uncle must have come in. Her guess was proven correct when he waltzed into the kitchen with Mercy hanging off of him like a little spider monkey.

"There's my girl. I was hoping I didn't miss you," Reggie said to Kiara as he came to kiss her temple and give her a hug. Kiara looked up into his handsome cinnamon toned face and gave him a huge grin. Reggie stood at about six-foot-one and was in shape for his age. And though he acted modestly, he was always dressed to the nines.

"Nope, wanted to help Lisa straighten up before we headed back home. Where you been?" Kiara nosily asked.

He was rarely late for a family get together, but he'd missed the entire dinner. He looked away before he chuckled so she knew he had to have been with a woman.

"Minding my business, little girl, that's where I been," Reggie answered before he squeezed Mercy to him and sat at the table. Kiara playfully rolled her eyes at him before catching up with him as Mercy played on his phone. Lisa joined them twenty or so minutes later and seemed more upbeat than she was when Rodrick left hours before.

"Hey, sis. I see your man is gone?" Reggie asked her knowingly. Everyone around the Atkins family knew how Rodrick was whether they agreed with his behavior or not.

"Yep, RJ, Rodney, and Rico went with him, too."

"Um. Did he say where they were going?"

"No. And I didn't ask, Reg."

"Lisa, you can't keep let—"

"Reggie," Lisa said with finality. She looked at Kiara again before turning back to him.

"Just don't, okay?" She asked him softly, almost begging. They stared at each other a few seconds before he clenched his jaw and nodded his head once.

Kiara looked down at her watch and saw it was almost six in the evening. The family always ate early on Sundays so dinner was usually over before the sun even started to set. She knew Mercy would hound her when they left about getting her nails done so she figured she should go ahead and leave.

"Well, me and this one are gonna take off," Kiara said as she got up. Mercy saw her move and immediately started to wiggle out of Reggie's lap, hugged Lisa's legs, and ran to the living room.

"Thanks so much for bringing her to see us, Kiara. She's always a doll," Lisa said as she hugged Kiara to her. She didn't know why, but Kiara felt compelled to hug her a little tighter and a little longer than usual. Lisa tensed at first, but relaxed into the hug and hugged her back just as tightly before releasing a breath and kissed Kiara's cheek.

"Come on, I'll walk you out. I'll be back in to get a plate, Lisa," Reggie said before he scooped Mercy from in front of the door and walked towards Kiara's Audi.

"Let me know when you make it," Reggie said after making sure Mercy was strapped in. Kiara nodded before starting the car.

"Uncle?" she said. He turned back towards her with his eyebrows raised in question. "Make sure she's okay for me."

Reggie gave her a sad smile before turning back towards the house. Kiara shook her head before putting her car in drive and started down the road.

"Let's go get our nails done, mama," she said to Mercy who yelled her excitement and put a smile back on Kiara's face.

2

MORIAH

"I don't get why we can't just eat at your house tonight, Der," Moriah said to her boyfriend Derrick.

"Because I'd like to take my woman out for a change if that's okay," he responded calmly while she just rolled her eyes. It was Friday evening and Moriah was exhausted but she was hungry so she'd go along for the ride, this time.

After undergrad and graduate school at Northwestern University, Moriah found her dream job as a clinical mental health counselor in one of the top private firms in the city. At first, she wanted to just do social work, but after learning more about counseling, she knew it was where she belonged.

Being as young as she was, she did need help getting an interview from connections she'd made from school, but once her boss saw what she had to offer and how the work was personal to her, she easily got the job and was making close to six figures after only a year of work.

With that being said, Moriah was tired and needed a break. Dealing with adolescents that needed help mentally and emotionally five days out of the week definitely wasn't for the weak.

Moriah and Derrick had been in a relationship for the past year and it was going fairly well. It took some time for Moriah to get over what her ex, Terrance, had done to her. She still went to her therapy sessions, but it wasn't as often and they were mostly just check ups to make sure she was handling life okay.

Derrick also worked at the facility that Moriah did, but as an accountant. He flirted with her for a few months before finally asking her out to lunch and they'd been together since.

They pulled into the parking lot of a hibachi restaurant downtown. Moriah turned towards her window and let out a breath of annoyance. Sometimes she wished they could just go to a burger joint and sit outside and chill out, but Derrick wasn't that type of man.

She wouldn't quite say he was pretentious, but he definitely liked to put on for others. Moriah grew up with money so she didn't care that much about it, but it was like Derrick had to make it known that he had it and wanted to show it off to her, when really, all she cared about was how he treated her.

She stepped out of his coupe and waited for him to come around to her side. He came to take her hand and kissed her cheek as he led her inside. In her heels, Moriah stood a little taller than Derrick but it didn't bother her since she knew she was a decent height for a woman, plus she knew not every man could be as tall as the ones in her family. She knew it got to him though, so she had switched out her heels for some cute flats she kept in her purse.

Derrick was dark skinned, a beautiful tone of deep walnut, with a bald head and a thick beard that came well past his chin. His eyes drooped as if he were sleepy or high all the time, but it added something special to his face, in her eyes, at least. He'd had orthodontic work done in his teen years and still wore a retainer at night to keep his teeth in line. He was handsome to her and she sometimes found herself looking at his profile as he slept, worked, or watched television beside her. He was on the skinnier side, but it worked for him so she didn't mind.

Once they were seated, Derrick started talking about his day and asked her about hers. This was their routine when they were together. It wasn't overly exciting but it was stable and she loved that about their relationship. When the waitress came to take their drink order, she noticed she ogled Derrick for more time than she should have but Moriah didn't say anything. For one, she knew her man was attractive and for two, she was confident and felt secure in her position in his life.

"So honey, I was thinking," Derrick started as he cut into his sushi and looked up at her. "We should take a little vacation somewhere."

"I thought you said you'd be too busy to go anywhere for a while, though," Moriah responded. She'd been trying to convince him to take a mini vacation for a few months, but he always gave an excuse as to why they couldn't.

"I know, but it seems like I'll have a little free time from work since I'm training a new accountant and I want to take you somewhere."

"That's great then, babe. That actually works out perfectly because we could take a trip to New York and finish with watching my cousin play ball. The Falcons play the Giants soon so it'll kill two birds with one stone," Moriah said as she gave him a dimpled grin.

"Sounds good," he forced out with a smile. Derrick had

never told her, but she had a feeling that he wasn't a big fan of the young Jackson men and she was pretty sure he was a little scared of her dad and uncle.

When her family first met Derrick, Renee and Kam seemed to like him, but the men weren't his biggest fans. Mordecai and Micah never came right out and said they didn't like him, but she could tell. The boys though, let their feelings be known.

Baby told her that he acted like he had a stick up his ass and Siah told her that he needed some hair on his chest or something because he could barely look them in their eyes. It was nothing worse to Jackson men than men not looking them in the eye while they were talking. Even though Chi had never met him, off the word of Baby and Siah, he also determined that Moriah "could do better."

The feelings were definitely mutual though because Derrick would avoid seeing them if he could. He'd never out right said it, but she could tell from how he'd framed certain things that he thought the boys were a little too hood for him to converse with and even though Siah was a little better, he'd rather not talk to him at all.

She didn't like it, but she'd just have to hope things would get better. Pushing them to the back of her mind, she continued to eat her food and talk to her man. She needed this.

～

"HIT me again and we are fighting, little girl," Moriah threatened her niece.

She almost laughed but stopped herself when she saw the unbothered look Mercy gave her before she hit her thigh again and ran off to sit on Baby's lap.

"It's frightening how much of her daddy she has in her without even meeting him," Senai said as she laughed at Mercy jumping at Baby.

"Who you tellin'," Moriah answered before turning fully to her best friend and staring at her.

"What is it?" Senai's light voice asked.

"I see you didn't bring Ren with you. Wonder why."

"He took up another shift so he had to hurry back home. What's your excuse?"

"I didn't want him feeling uncomfortable so I told Dee he didn't have to come," Moriah said as she shrugged her indifference.

"Um hmm. Probably just didn't want lover boy to see you undressing Mr. Andrews with your eyes."

"Bitch," Moriah deadpanned. "Fuck you, okay? I don't undress him with my eyes. I just like looking at him. Sometimes."

"Sometimes, my butt," Senai said with a chuckle. "If King is anywhere around, you'd know first with how hard you check for him."

"Oh? You mean how you are if my cousin is anywhere within a twenty mile radius of you?" Moriah asked just to get no response. "Exactly. Punk."

"Shut up. Anyway, Warren has been really tired lately. I've had to go see him more often than him coming here. And..."

"What is it?"

"He's gonna pop the question soon," Senai said quietly as she looked around to make sure no one heard her.

"He what?" Moriah shrieked. She asked so loudly, that those close to her turned to see what the problem was but she waved them off while never moving her eyes from Senai, who was wringing her hands.

"I overheard a conversation he was having with his mother the last time I went to visit. He told her he was going to ask when I finished school next semester. He's gonna ask Grammy soon and then get everything together. What the hell am I gonna do?"

Moriah knew she was freaking out because it was rare for Senai to curse. She didn't know how to feel about the situation, though, so she understood her friend's angst. Before she could say anything, Baby walked over to them and sat beside Senai with Mercy coming to sit on her lap. Mercy never liked sitting alone and if she could find someone else to sit on, she would.

"We are going out tonight and y'all ain't allowed to say no, so tell your punk ass nigga no he can't come and you tell goody two scrubs that you won't be able to call until late," Baby said with finality as he looked at Moriah and then at Senai before he got up and walked back towards the men.

"Well. Guess we're going out," Moriah sighed as she tickled Mercy.

"Let me get another tequila sunrise, please," Moriah told the bottle girl.

They'd been at the lounge for roughly an hour and it was getting more and more crowded every minute. They were in VIP but could see the floor and Moriah was glad she wasn't a part of the crowd.

She looked around and saw Baby with some random in his lap, Zeus' hand around some girl's neck while he whispered in her ear, Lord and King bobbing their heads to the music, and Ryan letting some girl in a dress that was way too tight grind on him. Moriah, Senai, Kiara, and Kiara's best friend Andrea were all sitting together and watching their environment and enjoying the vibe.

"Y'all look!" Andrea yelled out to them. They all looked

up and Moriah's eyes widened when she saw a small group of men walk up on Baby and Zeus.

"Aye. You need to get the fuck off my bitch, my nigga," one of the guys snapped as he looked in disdain at Baby. He looked upset with his fists clenched, but Baby looked unperturbed as he looked up at the man.

"Alright. How about you and the rest of The Temptations step back and you can get your lady," Baby calmly told him but his statement made Zeus and the rest of the boys holler with laughter. All the men were dressed similarly with different colored Polo shirts, dark jeans, and Jordans. It was strange for grown men to match but the group had it together.

"How 'bout you make me, nigga," the guy gritted out. Baby glanced over to Zeus who wore a teasing smile and then looked over to the girls; Senai looked worried while Moriah was sure her face matched Andrea and Kiara who had looks of anticipation on their faces. It was rare they ever saw someone step to any of the Jackson men.

Baby closed his eyes for a second before tapping the girl that was still on his lap on her thigh. Moriah found it crazy that she hadn't gotten up on her own even though her man was in her face. The girl lifted off of him and Baby stood to his full six-foot-three height.

The man looked even more agitated, probably not thinking Baby was that tall sitting down. Especially since he was maybe only six feet even, if that. Baby buttoned his suit jacket and stepped closer to the man who anxiously glanced at his boys behind him, who also looked a little frantic as Zeus, Lord, King, and Ryan also stood and were ready for action, all of whom were roughly the same height or taller than Baby.

"I will ask you again. *Please.* Step away from me and my

people and go on about your night," Baby said calmly. The VIP's DJ had subtly turned the music down and people could strain to hear what was going on. The man clenched his jaw and looked around and saw a lot of eyes on them. Eyes and whispering.

Moriah knew then that the man didn't want to be punked in front of a crowd so he'd probably do something stupid. Her thoughts were proven correct when the man told Baby to fuck himself and shoved him. Baby laughed before pulling out a gun and shooting him in his knee cap. All you could hear in the club were his screams and the bass of the music from the bottom floor.

Since Baby had his silencer on his gun, not many people heard the shot but those that had been paying attention to the altercation early on did notice the man screaming and the blood leaking from his leg. People started to panic and run out of the VIP section while their small group didn't move at all. The Jacksons knew the club owner personally since he was a family friend so they weren't worried about leaving or getting into any trouble.

The guy's friends tried to take off too, but were grabbed before they could. When the VIP section was clear, Baby fixed his suit and looked down at the man who was now crying and holding his wounded leg.

"Obviously you don't know who I am so I won't kill you today, but I need you to listen to me. The next time you walk up on somebody with the intention of intimidation, learn who the person is first because the next time, you won't be so lucky. Also," Baby turned, most likely looking for the girl that was the reason behind the altercation, but she was nowhere around.

"Find you a girl that would at least help you off the ground when you do something stupid. I'm letting you go, but know this. I can have every little detail of your lives by the time you get home tonight and won't lose a wink of sleep killing every single person you love if you try some get back shit. I put that on the Jackson name."

When Baby said Jackson, Moriah could have sworn she heard the guy on the floor whimper a little before he nodded his head vehemently. Baby stared at him for a few seconds and moved his head to the side, dismissing him and his little posse. The other men grabbed their friend and helped him limp down the stairs. The group was quiet for a moment before everyone laughed and got back to drinking. Moriah could do nothing but shake her head at her crazy family.

3

SIAH

"I think that'll work out best for you. Their contract seems like you'll get the most money long term instead of right away but it's not like you need it right away, anyway," Siah's friend-turned-agent Ty Boudreaux stated.

Siah wanted to keep business separate from personal relationships but he saw just how good of an agent Ty was and couldn't stop himself from getting with him. Since then, he'd made almost one hundred and twenty million dollars off of endorsements, business endeavors, and his football contract.

"Perfect," Siah said as he grinned big. "I'll get my lawyers on that so I can get that squared away. What you got goin' on this weekend?"

"I found a lil baddie I plan on taking out on Friday before I go back home," Ty smirked at him.

"Here you go," Siah playfully chuckled. "Don't know how you don't have a few beige kids running around."

"Shit, a lot of prayer and hell of a lot of luck."

They both laughed because he really was lucky. Ty loved

women, probably more than Baby did and he more often than not only dated Black women. He didn't care if they were American, African or even Caribbean, he needed his women to have melanin. It wasn't a fetish either since he'd been attracted to women of color since he was a kid and he always treated them as queens. Their friends always joked about Ty being "light-skinned white" and even though it was stupid, the description fit him well.

"Aight, I gotta get outta here. I have a meeting with two Braves and a Falcon today. Hopefully, they decide to join ya boy's team," Ty told Siah as he stood and straightened his dress shirt. He'd gone without a suit jacket since it was a warmer day so his tattoos were peeking from the top of his collar.

"That's cool, bro. I gotta get outta here myself and go get some food," Siah said as he also stood and slapped hands with Ty as they went their separate ways.

Siah cruised the Atlanta streets with a content smile on his face. Life for him was good. He'd led his team to three Super Bowls and had won two of them. He didn't want to play football for much longer, but he wanted to win at least one more big game before he retired from the game altogether and he knew he could with the team he had behind him.

He was still close as ever to his family and his play sister LaShea. The only thing lacking in his life at the moment was having a woman on his arm. He'd tried dating again, but no one stuck for long. He just couldn't connect with anyone long term and he hadn't felt real feelings for anyone in years.

His thoughts paused as he looked down at his phone when he saw a call coming through and connected to his bluetooth so he could talk.

"I am literally on my way, Shea," Siah said before LaShea could say anything to him.

"Shut up, I know you're on your way. I need you to stop somewhere for me, though."

"Man, where yo nigga at? He can't go?"

"Nope. That's what you get for being late. Stop and get some ice and wine. Thanks, brother," Shea said before hanging up on him. Siah let off a few curses before turning into a gas station so he could get some ice. He luckily was already bringing wine.

While standing in line to pay for the ice, he saw a woman out of the corner of his eye that had him turning fully to watch her. She wasn't that tall compared to him, maybe five-foot-six or five-foot-seven, but her legs looked long and the way her hips widened had him looking at her closely. She had a pretty caramel complexion with a button nose, thick lips, and cat-like eyes. Her hair was in a tight bun on top of her head with a long bang that hung near her eyes. When he finished paying for the ice, he looked around the store but didn't see her, so he rushed outside and caught her getting into a silver Acura.

"Excuse me," Siah said as he came to a stop in front of her car door. Up close, she was even prettier than he thought. She turned to him and looked him up and down before answering him.

"Yes?" she answered. Her voice was husky, like she'd have the perfect phone sex voice. Siah cleared his throat to get his thoughts together.

"My name is Messiah Jackson and I just wanted to let you know that I find you to be amazingly beautiful," Siah told her as he stared intently at her. So intently that she had to look away. He was disappointed, but only briefly before she responded to him.

"Well, Mr. Messiah Jackson, my name is Sharell Lowry and I think you are incredibly handsome."

"So handsome you'd be willing to give me your number?"

She looked at him for a few moments before a small smile came across her face.

"Yeah. I think I'd be willing to do that."

"Took you long enough to get here," LaShea chastised him with a raised lip as she answered her door. Siah just mushed her face and walked into her townhome.

He turned into the living room and saw his teammate Avery watching tv with sweats and a wife beater on. He must have just finished grilling because he hated wearing a real shirt when he had to be in smoke.

"Damn, finally. You know her ass gets cranky as hell when she can't eat on time," Avery said as he got up and dapped Siah.

Turns out, it was Avery texting LaShea all those years ago at Dave & Busters. He'd gone to see her at her job a few times before finding the nerve to ask her out to a four o'clock-in-the-morning coffee date where they got to know each other better. They kept their relationship a secret until LaShea could tell he was actually serious about them being together, but the privacy didn't last long because Avery wanted the world to know about his woman.

They'd been going strong for about three years officially and were what a lot of people called relationship goals. Avery was still working on getting LaShea to move in with him, but she was being her usual stubborn self about it.

At first, Siah wasn't so sure about them being together because he knew what came with being a professional athlete, but after having a serious talk with Avery, he knew his friend was all about LaShea and had been stuck since the first night he'd seen her.

"Come on here, Rylan. I'm hungry," LaShea called from the kitchen. She'd started calling Siah by his middle name a few years prior and never stopped. He knew arguing with her about it was futile since she'd just ignore him anyway so he'd accepted it some time ago.

The three of them sat down at her dining room table and ate and joked around. Siah didn't have any real family in Atlanta, but he had a few people that were just as close.

"Mo, are you sure you wanna come? You know how your boy is," Siah said to Moriah. She was telling him of her plans to come to New York around the time he had to play the Giants. He didn't doubt she wanted to come and see him play, but her boyfriend was iffy and he didn't think he'd be with it.

"Siah, shut up. Yes, I'm sure. It'll be fine," she responded. She said it like she was trying to convince herself just as much as she was trying to convince him.

"Alright, fine. I'll put in for you to get a couple of tickets. You wanna sit in a box or what?"

"You know I don't do boxes unless it's freezing cold. It'll be mid October though, so we should be good."

"Um hmm, I hear you," Siah said. She might be good, but her sadity boyfriend might feel differently.

They spoke a few more minutes about what all she planned to do on her vacation before he decided to ask about his Bratz doll. She was still a sore subject for him seeing as he never stopped loving her, even after all these years.

He'd tried to move on but no matter how many women he ended up conversing with, he always ended up comparing them to *her* and they always fell short. His mind went to Sharell and he hoped she'd be the one to clear his thoughts for a little while.

"She's...fine," Moriah answered hesitantly.

"That means she's not. What's goin' on?"

"Well, you know she's graduating next semester and she's just stressed because she doesn't know where to do her residency. She can stay here or she can go somewhere else. I wanna be selfish and tell her to keep her ass here, but I don't wanna do that. Plus, Warren..."

"What about him?" Siah asked quickly. He never said *his* name. He felt if he didn't say his name, he wouldn't be as important. Some days, it worked for him. Other days, his denial still felt bitter on his tongue.

"It's just the distance and other things. Nothing too serious for now," Moriah hurriedly said. Siah knew something was off, but he didn't speak on it.

Before he could continue, he saw he had a call and a huge smile covered his face.

"Aye, Mo. Let me holla at you later. Your brother is calling."

"Oh, okay. Tell him Daddy said he needs to call him in the morning. He has something to discuss with him," she said before telling Siah she loved him and hung up. Siah clicked over and heard Chi yelling at somebody in the background.

"Damn, nigga. I get you still running shit in there, but you gotta do that in my ear?" Siah fussed at his cousin.

"Shut yo ass up. What's up with you, though?" Chi asked.

"Ain't shit. Just got to the crib a little while ago. What yo ass doin'?" Siah said.

"Just got off the phone with Baby checking on things and making sure he's straight."

Chi making sure Baby was straight was an understatement. Even though he was in a maximum security prison an hour outside of Chicago, Chi was still running their organization with an iron fist.

He had it made in prison with a cell phone and laptop inside and just about all the guards were on their payroll as well. He was treated like a king and it was like he never left the outside world. He had it so well that he had Kiara come see him much more often than what should have been possible and though illegal, had plenty of conjugal visits. He made sure she was taken care of in every way.

They talked for ten or so more minutes before Chi said he had to call Mercy for her goodnight story. Siah delivered Moriah's message of calling Mordecai the next day and they hung up after saying their farewells. Siah went to his kitchen to find a snack, but on his way to the refrigerator, his phone dinged with a text that put a smirk on his face.

Sharell: Hi, figured I'd text u first

Siah: Thank you for texting me. I was waiting on you to hit me up.

Sharell: Well here I am. Wassup?

Siah: Shit. Just chillin and eating. What you up to?

Sharell: Kinda bored actually. Let's do somethin

Siah paused and thought for a minute. He'd been thinking about Sharell for the past week or so but didn't know if he wanted to go there with her. He was obviously attracted to her looks but didn't know if it was anything more than that. He figured that night could be the time to find out.

Siah: Bet. Send me your address and I'll come scoop you. I'll take you out.

Sharell: Ok :) Coming to you now

Siah got up from the bench at the foot of his bed and went to his closet to find something to put on. He took a deep sigh. Maybe Sharell could be the missing piece he needed.

4

SENAI

"Ahhh, Warren," Senai cooed. She had her eyes closed tightly with her hands tangled in his sheets. Warren had her thick thighs on his shoulders with his face buried between them.

"Let go, baby," Warren murmured before putting his lips back on her center. Senai's legs shook as she released and he kissed her inner thighs gently until she calmed down.

He climbed her body after putting on a condom and entered her slowly as he kissed her lips. Senai closed her eyes as she enjoyed their time together. She loved when he made love to her, but sometimes, she wished he could switch things up.

She'd mentioned it before, but he'd always say he couldn't treat her roughly or change up too much because he liked what he liked during sex. Their intimate times were never bad so she made due with what they shared.

Twenty minutes later, Senai was in the shower and deep in her thoughts. She was heading back to Chicago soon so she had to get herself together. After washing her body a few times, she stepped out of Warren's huge shower, lotioned her body, and got dressed. Her hair was braided in plaits she'd take down later to have some extra curl, but for the time being were sitting in a bun on top of her head.

"I fixed us a little something, baby," Warren said as she walked into the kitchen to get some coffee.

"Thank you," she answered softly as she leaned down to kiss under his ear.

They ate quietly and gave each other loving looks until Warren set his cell phone down on the table and gave her his full attention.

"I want you here with me, Senai," Warren stated and she huffed out her frustration.

"Warren—," she started but was cut off.

"No, Senai. Just hear me out. I know you're in your last year of school but after that, you can start fresh here in Wisconsin for residency. You know my hospital is the best one in the state. I can put in a good word for you. We've been together so long and I don't see the problem with you coming here to finish before we start the rest of our lives together."

"Warren, I didn't dictate where to do your residency. *You* decided to come back home so you could be closer to your parents. I love you, but when I get the call to go somewhere, *that's* when I'll decide where to go. And I don't need you to put in a good word. I got into med school without you, and I will continue on my path the same way. As you said, we've been together a long time, so a little while longer won't hurt anything," Senai confidently responded after a few moments of silence.

"Baby, we need to be together, especially now that I'm moving up in the eyes of the chief residents at the hospital. I'll be choosing my specialty soon and I know I'll be busier than ever. And who knows? As my wife, you might not even be a doctor for that long. If I was with someone else, they'd do what they needed to do to secure their spot with me," Warren said tensely. Warren wanted to be an orthopedic surgeon which would add time to him being under someone else's command before he could run the show.

"Well, you should understand that you're not with someone else. You're with me. And me? I'm not securing a thing. There will never be another me so if you think you threatening me with you leaving because I won't follow you scares me, you don't know me as well as I thought. I can't believe you said that to me," Senai softly spoke before rolling her eyes and getting up from the table and putting her dishes in the dishwasher before going to the bedroom to get her bag packed so she could leave. She didn't plan on leaving for another couple of hours, but the way Warren spoke to her made her want to leave early.

"Senai. Baby, I didn't mean anything by what I just said. I just need you to understand where I'm coming from, too," Warren told her as he walked into his bedroom and leaned against the wall.

"It's not about what you said, Ren. It's how you said it, and you know that. That isn't the first time you slickly said something like that, either. If you can't handle me being away from you, then leave me be. What you won't do though, is try and guilt me into coming here or threatening to be with someone else because of a career choice that both us made. I refuse to be put into that position," Senai said after packing her belongings and looking him in the eyes. He clenched his jaw and looked away before glancing back at her.

"I hear you, Senai. But, there's nothing wrong with needing me as well as your career, you know? I'm your man. You should want to be with me."

"Ren, let's not confuse things," Senai said as she walked to him and put her hand on his chest. "I do want you. I love you, but I love me, too. Just like you'll choose your career over me, I'll do the same. Remember that the next time you have the audacity to say I should choose you over me and my wants," Senai declared with a tilt of her head before she gave him a soft kiss in the corner of his mouth and walked out of his house.

~

"Hey, Grammy," Senai announced as she walked into her grandmother Althea's house.

"Good, you here. Go check my pie and if it's ready, put it on the counter for me," Althea said without looking away from the news.

Senai grumbled to herself but went to the kitchen. She saw the pie was ready so she took it out of the oven and set it on the counter. She walked back to the living room slowly before taking a seat on the loveseat and watched television with her grandmother for a few minutes before either of them spoke.

"What brings you by on a weekday? You normally don't come around 'til Saturday or Sunday," Althea said as she muted the news and turned her head towards Senai.

"Am I selfish, Grammy?" Senai asked hesitantly. She might have talked a good game at Warren's house a couple of days before, but the situation was still bothering her. By the expression on Althea's face, she could tell she caught her off guard.

"Selfish? Baby, you are probably one of the most unselfish people I've ever met. Where's this coming from?" Althea asked concernedly.

"You know I went to see Warren this past weekend. He wants me to follow him there after my white coat ceremony. And, I just don't know. Is that selfish of me?"

Althea glanced at Senai who was wringing her hands in nervousness. She gave her a small smile before she got up from her chair and let Senai know to follow her. They silently walked to the kitchen and Althea grabbed a knife from the drawer and cut both of them a nice slice of sweet potato pie. She put a scoop of vanilla ice cream on top for Senai and fixed a tall glass of milk for herself.

"Did you know that when your grandaddy Tibb and I met he was playing baseball at Jackson State? And he was good, too, real good. So good, that he was being scouted to go to the Minors. But, he met me. And like father like son, we ended up pregnant soon after," Althea said with a knowing smile that probably came from thinking of Senai's father that slowly slid from her face. "A lot of his family, especially his mama, friends and his coaches said he could take care of us from the road. That we'd be better off if he went ahead and played ball. Wanna guess what he did?"

"He didn't go?" Senai questioned quietly and Althea shook her head slowly.

"No, he didn't. It was different back then for Black folks. Harder and more challenging, especially down South. And marriage was different, too—as long as he took care of home, everything else would follow. After talking to his mama, I even tried to convince him that going might be the best, but he was hard headed and didn't wanna listen. So, we both finished school and I found a teaching job and he went to work at one of the plants in the area. His mama was so damned mad at him and me that I don't think she talked to us again for some years," Althea reminisced.

"Why'd he do that, though, Grammy? I know y'all would

have been more financially stable with him having a professional career."

Althea sat quietly for a few moments with a faraway
look on her face as her chocolate eyes grew glossy and
turned to Senai with a content smile.

"He wanted to be around for us. He wanted us set so
when he heard about a good job up here, we moved and my
husband provided for his family, but he was present, too. He
would have made real good money playing ball, but would
he have been there? My sons knew their daddy just as much
as I did. Who knows how their relationships would have
been if he was always on the road.

"He was selfish. Instead of doing what others wanted for
him, he did what *he* wanted, and went where *he* would be
happy."

Althea paused and grabbed Senai's hands that were on
the table beside her empty plate.

"If you being selfish means that you are happy, then be
selfish, baby. No one can live your life but you and if you're
not doing something that can make your life better, what's
the point? If that boy loves you, then he'd want that for you,
too."

Althea got up and put their dishes in the sink so she
could wash them later, and kissed Senai's forehead for a few
seconds before going back into the living room to finish
watching the news. Senai sat at the kitchen table and
exhaled before putting her head in her hands. She didn't
know what to do.

5

CHI

"We have the files you needed, Jackson," one of the guards told Chi as he sat in front of the library computer.

"Thank you, Ernie. You can just put them on the table," Chi responded without looking away from the computer screen.

When the police busted in on Chi that day, they found him with two kilos of cocaine in his hands. They'd received an anonymous tip of someone trafficking drugs through the residence and even though they found Chi with cocaine in his hands, they didn't find anything else.

Luckily, Chi had his lieutenants move their work and cash around the night before and whoever tipped the police off didn't know that. Chi was booked that day and was held without bond before finally being sentenced with possession and intent to sell and sentenced ten to twelve years but was able to get it reduced to seven to ten. God willing, he could get out early with good behavior in the next year or so.

Until then, Chi continued to be the kingpin he was. He

still made sure his guys did what they were supposed to. Baby, Zeus, and Lord handled everything he couldn't and the streets still knew who he was and how he got down.

Rumors of how he was set up went around the hood for a while but no solid stories ever came up. JJ, Ryan's soldier that called him that day, was killed sometime after he placed the call to Chi and was found with bullet holes littering his body on the block of the trap house two days after Chi was taken in.

Hank Franklin, one of the police captains on their payroll, let them know that the anonymous tip came from what sounded like a woman, but they never were able to find her. It's as if she vanished after making the call.

"Aye, Chi, let me talk to you for a minute," one of the prisoners called out as he walked up on Chi but was stopped short when another prisoner told him to wait. Mordecai made sure Chi was protected at all times, whether it be the officers or prisoners having his back.

"How can I help you today, Twitch?" Chi asked as he stood to his full height in front of the older man. Twitch got his name being a heavy user of anything he could get his hands on and had a permanent twitch in his hand and the right side of his face because of it.

"I'm tryna get a little somethin' off you," Twitch said. He couldn't look Chi in his eye and looked everywhere but his face. That already had Chi vexed.

"I ain't got it. Sorry," Chi said as he stepped past him. He stopped when he felt Twitch's clammy hand wrap around his forearm.

"You walkin' around here like you a king and you bleed just like me, lil nigga. You remember that the next time you walk away from one of us regular folks," Twitch gritted out before stomping off.

Chi looked to his left and saw his boy Tiny look at him with a raised eyebrow. Tiny definitely wasn't little at three hundred pounds and around Chi's height of six-foot-five. He'd graduated high school a few years before Chi, but they'd always been cool. When Chi was brought over, they clicked right away and he'd been by Chi's side since he'd been inside.

He wouldn't get out for another few years, but when he did, Chi already let him know he'd be taken care of for the rest of his life and had a job when he was ready. Chi gave him a subtle nod of the head which Tiny responded with a small smirk.

When they made it back to their cellblock a little more than an hour later, there was a scuffle outside of Chi's cell and a huge fight began. He stood on the inside of his cell and found Twitch's eyes and tilted his head before Twitch's face was met with multiple fists and three shanks to his side. As he was being carried away to the infirmary, Chi looked him dead in the eye and smiled as the guards tried to get everyone settled down. Chi went back to his bunk and lied down with his arms behind his head. *He had to have known better than threatening me. He must not know who my daddy is.*

"COME ON, bae. Send it for me. I ain't had it all week," Chi pleaded with Kiara over FaceTime.

"Mal, really? Your daughter is in the backseat asleep and you tryna get a video. Besides, it's Wednesday. I just came over that way on Sunday," she said with a roll of her eyes.

"Hell yeah, really and shit, that is a week. Have you seen you? I do need you to stop losing weight, though. Told you bout that shit," Chi said with a disapproving scowl.

Kiara told him how Moriah made her go to the gym more often since Senai was too busy with school to go with her. Because of that, Kiara was slimming down a little but still had her wide hips and ample behind. Her thighs were getting smaller though and Chi hated that.

"Shut up, boy. You act like I weigh a hundred pounds or something. I just went down a pants size."

"Yeah, aight. Let me find out you tryna get smaller than Sen and I'm busting outta here and fattening you up myself," Chi told her.

Moriah had a lot of butt and bigger breasts but was for the most part slim thick, whereas Senai had a huge butt, wide hips and thighs but had a tiny waist and small breasts. Kiara always told Chi that she wanted to be a little smaller like Senai, but he always said no because Senai was still too small for his liking.

"Whatever, Mal. Did you get the video of Ci-Ci I sent you?"

"You know I did. My baby can dance her little ass off. She got ballet today, right?"

"Uh huh. I'm about to drop her off at Mama's house and then I'm going to work and I'll pick her up from ballet when I'm done."

"Cool, make sure she calls me around seven, Ari. I should be good to go by then. If not, I'll let you know," Chi told Kiara.

They talked ten more minutes before Chi had to get off the phone because it was time to start his day. The cell doors slid open sometime later and the prisoners got up to get checked. When Ernie came into his cell to check, he handed him an envelope that had Chi raising his eyebrows in question.

"From the warden," Ernie whispered to which Chi

nodded and stuck the envelope under his undershirt so he could read it later.

Afterwards, Chi got his breakfast and went to the library where he worked every day. From there, he'd check his emails and get down to business with his lieus for the day. Halfway through the day, Chi received word that Twitch had died through the night from internal bleeding and he breathed easy. He hated having to take care of people on the inside, but he hated being disrespected more.

"What y'all got for me?" Chi asked, started his meeting. He had Baby, Ryan, Benny, and three other lieus on the video call. Even though they could only speak in coded messages, their meetings were always productive.

"So, all my treats are sold out. I got my kids making me some more and we'll be set for Halloween," Ryan spoke about being all out of work. It would be up to Baby to get more cut and sent out so they could get back on the streets.

"Benny, how are our bankers holding up? We had a deposit a couple of days ago. Any interest accumulated yet?" Chi asked Benny. Bankers were just code for their buyers and if money had been coming in well.

"Looks good. I'm actually thinking we can expand and get with a new bank in another area," Benny answered and Chi nodded his head in agreement.

"We can table it. Anything else pertinent to what we're talking about?" Chi asked and no one spoke up. "Cool. I'll get back at y'all later then. Baby, I'll call you later," Chi finished before everyone got off the call.

Chi continued working and called Baby back a few hours later to talk more about business. He was talking to a few people before he realized time had gotten away from him and it was almost time for his baby to call him.

He giddily went to his small office space in the library

and got set up. He remembered he had the note from the warden on him, and took out the envelope to open it. What he read had him excited and anxious for the coming months. Just as he was sitting down, a FaceTime call was coming through.

"Daddy!" Mercy exclaimed when she saw Chi's face. She still had on her gold leotard with her hair in a tight bun on top of her hair.

"Hey, baby girl. Daddy missed you. How was rehearsal?"

"So fun, Daddy. Ms. Crissy said we'll be ready for our show soon. It's gonna be at Grandaddy's contension center," Mercy told him excitedly. Her words were choppy but he understood what she was trying to get out.

"Convention center, baby."

"Yeah, that's what I said," Mercy said as her face frowned up which made her right dimple pop. Chi couldn't help but laugh because Mercy was going to have a smart mouth just like Kiara when she was older.

They talked for a little while longer, with Chi reading her a bedtime story, before Kiara got back on the phone. Chi rarely talked to Kiara after talking to Mercy and instead, just liked to be on the phone and watch her as if he were there enjoying her presence. Chi just looked at his wife and felt an immense amount of love for the woman that had stuck by his side through all the bad times.

"Hey, Ari," Chi softly spoke.

"Yeah?" Kiara responded as she looked up from the work she was doing.

"I love you."

"And I love you."

6

MICAH

"Reeny!" Micah called out as he came into the living room.

"Stop yelling, I'm right here," Renee said as she walked to meet him from the kitchen.

"Which one?" Micah asked as he held up two different colored ties.

Renee circled her husband as she looked at his light brown skin and solid body covered by a custom royal blue suit. She bit her lip in thought as she eyed the ties in his hands and pointed to the one in his right.

"That'll work," Renee said as she took the golden tie and put it on to tie it. Micah stared intently at her as she finished and he could tell she worked hard to keep the smile off of her face.

"Thanks, Reeny. What you doin' today?" Micah said as he pecked her and sat down at the island in the kitchen.

"I'm not sure. I wish I could get my girls to do something. They're just so grown now they rarely have any time for me anymore," Renee answered somberly while she put a plate in front of Micah to eat.

"Yeah, they're getting up there in age now, but I'm sure they wouldn't mind getting up with you today, mama. Have them come over and y'all have a girls' day. I'll have some masseuses and that nail bar send over some people for y'all. Get you some catered food? How about that?" Micah asked her. He hated seeing his wife sad because the kids were getting older and didn't want to be under her as much.

She gave him a smile that lit up her entire face and he knew that he'd do anything to keep that smile present so he told her he'd call to get everything set up for around noon so she, Moriah, Senai, Andrea, Kiara, and little Mercy could enjoy a day of pampering together.

After finishing his breakfast, Micah put on his shoes and kissed Renee goodbye before grabbing his wallet and keys and left their house. He and Mordecai were getting together with their lawyers to try and find a way to get Chi out of prison. Their lawyers believed they may have found something to help and they were anxious to get the news.

On the way to Mordecai's house, he placed a call to Kiara, who was his personal assistant, and had her set up their appointments with masseuses and nail technicians and told her to take off for the day. She argued with him for a few moments because she felt she needed to be there, but he finally convinced her that he wouldn't go bankrupt from them being away from the office for one Saturday.

"Damn nigga, took you long enough. Couldn't get up off sis for a day?" Mordecai joked as he jumped in Micah's ride.

"Fuck you, boy. Besides, she was on top," Micah said cheekily before the brothers cackled.

They rode downtown as they caught up until they pulled into the parking lot of the law firm that represented them. Though it was Saturday, they were still able to meet with the attorneys that had represented their family for over two decades.

When they made it to the twelfth floor, they told the overzealous receptionist who they were there for. She'd, for some reason, thought it wise to openly flirt with Micah whose temper was worse than his older brother's when pushed.

"You accidentally touch me again and I'll accidentally shoot off your pinky. I'm not the one, little girl," Micah calmly told her. Mordecai snickered at his brother and Micah gave him a long look in return. Her eyes bulged as her ivory skin took a pinkish hue. She placed the call to her boss who showed up not two minutes later and led them to the conference room.

"Well, gentlemen," Scott, one of their attorneys, spoke as they all settled in. "One of our paralegals reviewed your son's files and took a longer look at the first warrant that was given. It doesn't match the one the courts provided us later on."

"Whoa, wait. So are you saying it was foul play?" Mordecai asked. Micah could tell he was getting excited but was schooling his features.

"That's definitely what it seems like. The story behind the narcotics division who did the bust is also sketchy. They've been tight lipped all this time, but one of the captains for that precinct is set to retire in a few months and that would be the most effective time to start asking questions again."

The second attorney, Scott's brother Arnold, handed them copies of both warrants and they could see it had been tampered with. If they could only find out who'd given the tip, Micah knew it would answer a lot of questions. They spoke with their lawyers for another hour before leaving.

The atmosphere was tense with excitement and anxiety but neither man spoke until they got back into Micah's truck.

"I don't think we need to tell the boys about this just yet, but I think we need to get back in these streets and get some answers. Some real answers," Micah started.

"Yeah, you might be right, brother. Time for D-Mor and Jackie Boy to make a reappearance," Mordecai responded with a mischievous glint in his eye. Micah could do nothing but laugh because he hadn't been called Jackie Boy in ten plus years but it seemed like the other side, the ruthless side, was about to show up again.

Micah made it back home hours later, tired and mentally exhausted. He and Mordecai had searched high and low for any snitches or fiends that may have seen something four years ago but they came up short once again.

Whoever set Chi up had to have planned it out meticulously and covered their tracks well. Mordecai didn't want to, but Micah was close to having King come in to hear the 9-1-1 call and see if he could isolate and locate anything about the mystery woman's voice. If they could just find her, they'd be one step closer to getting justice for Chi and getting him back to the real world.

He stepped into his living room to find his tables, couches, and chairs pushed to the wall to make room for massage tables and room for the nail techs to have their way. He stared in astonishment because he didn't think it was going to be a full-on spa in his house, but his woman looked relaxed and content so that was all that mattered. He was about to slide down the hall unseen but heard the squeal of a child before feeling something knock into his legs.

"Uncle! Hi!" Mercy grinned up to him, looking just like her aunt Moriah at her age. She was in an overalls dress with her hair piled on top of her head and when he looked at her tiny hands, her nails were painted a bright yellow, which was her favorite color, just like her aunt Senai, who'd convinced her the color made her dark brown skin "pop" like no other color could.

"Hey, munchkin," Micah said to her as he picked her up and she squealed with excitement. Just like Moriah, she loved crawling all over him and wasn't settled until she was sitting on top of his shoulders; thank goodness for tall ceilings. He walked into the kitchen holding on to her legs and went to get ice cream for the both of them. Even though he didn't eat many desserts, he knew his grand niece had a sweet tooth and couldn't tell her no when she asked to eat "banilla" ice cream with him.

"Is Grandaddy coming? I didn't see him today," she asked with big hazel eyes and ice cream all over her mouth. Micah laughed lightly before getting a paper towel and wetting it so he could clean her up when she was done.

"Let me call him and tell him you're here. I'm sure he'll come right over," Micah told her as he pulled out his cell phone to call his brother. He placed the call and let her know he'd be there soon.

By the time Mercy was finishing her ice cream, the ladies were finishing up in the living room and showing their guests out. Renee walked into the kitchen and sauntered to him before she placed a sweet kiss on his lips. She settled between his legs with a lazy smile.

"You better now?" He asked lowly in her ear to which she just nodded slowly. He squeezed her thigh and looked at his family that was walking slowly into the kitchen with similar looks to his wife.

"Guess my money was well spent today," he joked as Kiara, Moriah, Senai, and Andrea all came to give him a kiss on the cheek and sat in the kitchen to eat some ice cream as well. The only one that was missing was Kam, but she was in Brooklyn visiting her sister for the week. They talked and joked as Mordecai walked into the house with his spare key and picked up an excited Mercy and showered her with kisses.

"Dang, Daddy. Am I invisible now?" Moriah asked with fake anger. Micah chuckled because he knew she felt some type of way about not being the apple of her father's eye anymore.

"Girl, please. I just saw your white ass yesterday and all you wanted was some money," Mordecai teased as he mushed Moriah. Moriah smacked her lips as everyone laughed.

Everyone thought Chi was as bright as his kids would be, but Moriah had him beat. Her skin was so fair, she could literally pass as white if she tried, but her Afrocentric features definitely gave her true heritage away.

"Hilarious," Moriah responded flatly. As they continued their conversation, Micah and Mordecai both received a text at the same time and as he read the text, Micah's hand tightened around Renee's thigh; she looked back at him with a concerned expression.

"You gotta go?" Renee asked quietly. He responded with a head nod and kissed her quickly before moving her gently to the side so he could stand.

Micah and Mordecai looked at each other and walked to his spare room and locked the door. Neither of them spoke as they both dressed in all black. The brothers always left emergency clothing at each other's homes for situations such as this one.

After they were dressed, Micah grabbed his duffle bag of toys and they went through the garage without telling the girls goodbye. He sent Renee a message of love and let her know he didn't know what time he'd be back in before they jumped on the highway to their parents' home to pick up their father. He'd let them in on some intriguing information he'd found out and it was time to act.

"Let's go catch a rat, brother."

7
____

MORDECAI

Mordecai stood in the corner of the room breathing heavily as he stared with contempt at the man that was strapped down. He looked up at his brother who sat cooler than a fan on the other side of the room and got frustrated all over again.

They'd been in their blood room all morning with the man Isaiah found out was connected to Chi's imprisonment. It was the sixth day they'd had him and Mordecai had been beating him senseless, but he wasn't budging and Mordecai was starting to get annoyed.

"You done yet?" Micah had the nerve to ask as if he were bored and Mordecai sucked his teeth in response. He flipped him off and went to take a seat.

"Great. Let's get to work, shall we?" Micah asked sardonically. When Micah got into his Jackie Boy persona, it sent chills down Mordecai's spine. His brother was a different breed and it scared even him at times.

Mordecai watched as Micah, who was still fully clothed in his suit, took four different blades from his bag of toys. Mordecai only shook his head because he knew how much his brother loved his knives and torturing someone by cutting and slicing skin wasn't how he wanted to get answers initially; it appeared that the time had come.

"Mister Daniel Murphy, is it? It seems we've reached an impasse. We want some information about what happened four years ago on the afternoon of May 22 and clearly, you're pretty tight lipped about it. So where does that leave us?"

The man started to breathe heavily after Micah calmly asked his question as if he knew what was coming. When he didn't answer, Micah shook his head in mock sympathy and walked closer to him as he held the first blade in his hand and twirled it through his fingers like a professional. Mordecai cracked an amused smile as he nodded to continue when Micah looked over at him with big pleading eyes.

Before the man could say anything, Micah drove the knife through his forearm. The blade was so sharp, it made a clean cut through his skin and since Micah was always accurate, the knife didn't hit the bone. Micah allowed the man to scream out his pain for about fifteen seconds before slapping him and telling him to quiet down and walked back towards the table to get another knife. Mordecai chuckled at his brother's theatrics but knew they could finally get real answers; he figured he'd play good cop for a moment.

"Well, Danny Boy, looks like you're in a bit of a pickle. Now, I can help you avoid Freddy Kreuger over there, but only if you give me something good," Mordecai said to the now snot-nosed man. If he was crying from a little stab wound, he'd be out of his mind by the time Micah was done with him.

"Okay, okay. I'll tell you. Just keep that crazy nigga away

from me!" he begged. Mordecai hid his smile and nodded, knowing Daniel wasn't leaving alive.

"That day, my cousin called me and told me I had to do somethin' for him. I owed him a favor so I had to help but I swear I ain't want to," he started and Mordecai just nodded his head to get him to continue.

"He-he said that I needed to go to that trap and take out the uppity nigga that holds it down and when I get done to make a call," he said.

"Who did you make the call to?" Mordecai asked him, happy that the story was slowly coming together.

"I just knew the name was Ivy. They didn't say nothin' when I called, but sent a text and told me to make the nigga call who was in charge to come runnin'. When he made the call, I knocked him out and dropped him off where I was told. That's it," he swore.

Mordecai looked over to Micah who was sitting at the table with a knife in his hand twirling it around. He had a somber expression on his face that made Mordecai bite down on his molars hard. They figured it was someone who had it out for them, but the plan seemed well thought out. It was a bigger deal than they thought. They needed to get to the bottom of it.

"Who is your cousin, Daniel?" Mordecai asked.

"I-I can't," he started but was interrupted by Mordecai.

"If you can't, then ain't shit else we need to talk about," Mordecai answered as he signaled Micah to finish him off.

"No! No, just wait! Just promise me Ima be able to leave here," he begged.

Micah looked at Mordecai and nodded his head in agreement.

"Fine. Now tell me who your cousin is."

"Street. His name Terrance Rhodes, but he go by Street."

Mordecai closed his eyes for a split second before releasing a long breath. When he opened them he looked at his brother with a dangerous look and that was all it took before Micah threw his knife and hit Daniel squarely in his chest. He was in so much shock and pain, that he couldn't even scream, but let out a pained groan.

"You-you said I could leave. You promised," he winced out.

"And you will. I just never said you'd leave alive," Mordecai told him before another knife punctured the left side of his chest and he wheezed before taking his last breath.

"How the fuck did the nigga even get shit together to set him up? He was already locked up by the time they snatched Chi," Micah angrily asked Mordecai as he came to stand beside him and looked down at the body in front of them with disgust.

"I don't know, but we gotta figure it out. I know which prison he's at so I gotta make some calls. One step closer, though," Mordecai answered, releasing another breath.

"One step closer."

⌒

"Thanks for the help, Pop. There's no way we woulda been able to find that dude hiding out in Detroit," Mordecai told Isaiah as they sat in Isaiah's office drinking cognac later that evening.

"You know I do what I can to help my boys. Besides, your mama call herself giving me the damn silent treatment since she said I wasn't trying hard enough to get her baby outta jail," Isaiah joked as he puffed on his cigar.

"Glad she got you by the balls then, old man. Who

found him for you, though?" Mordecai asked as he sipped from his glass.

"One of Baby's ghosts actually. I've been helping the boy mature and he came to me about hearing some things since he didn't want to upset Baby if he could help it. Next thing I know, kid done pulled up to the gate with the nigga in his trunk," Isaiah laughed out while Mordecai was silent with shock. He didn't even know Baby had spies in their other locations. He knew his sex dolls were there, but now he was intrigued on what else his nephew had going on.

"Damn, Pop. Am I that far removed from the game?"

"Hell yes. And you need to stay that way. When we retire, we retire, son. We're here to assist and that's it. Malachi getting caught up in some get back shit is a horrible situation, but shit doesn't change. We just adapt. We raise the next generation to take over and take over is what they've done. You've given more than enough to the game, baby boy. Enjoy being out," Isaiah spoke firmly but lovingly to his oldest.

They sat in silence as they sipped and smoked. Mordecai was deep in thought when he figured he'd talk to his dad about something else that had been heavy on his mind.

"Spit it out, Eloi," Isaiah said as he set his glass on the small table in front of them.

"You remember when Ronnie died?" Mordecai asked lowly, looking into his glass and avoiding his father's gaze. He felt Isaiah sit up in his chair so he could pay full attention to what he was going on about.

"Of course. It was a rough time for you," he replied.

"It was. It was even worse because I lost two of my loves instead of just one."

Isaiah didn't say anything so Mordecai looked up at his father and found his eyes already on him. The hazel eyes he'd inherited were low but filled with understanding and love. Isaiah nodded his head for him to continue so he took a deep breath and did so.

"Ronnie set me up a little after we found out how bad the cancer really was. She didn't want me to be alone," Mordecai chuckled bitterly. He was still so angry at how life had a way of humbling you. "She set me up with a woman that I ended up falling for, but the guilt got to me and I let her go."

"Let me guess. You miss Selena and want her back?" Isaiah asked after listening to Mordecai vent his frustrations. After hearing her name, Mordecai looked sharply at his father.

"Don't give me that look, D. Ronnie told Emma about the girl and of course ya mama wanted to check her out. She couldn't do that without me finding out, so she mentioned it to me. I didn't get in it 'cause you didn't come to me about it, but you know how Emma is so she met the girl and they hit it off. Hell, I don't wanna make you feel bad, but she liked the Selena girl more than Ronnie for you," Isaiah said casually like he hadn't just dropped a few bombs.

"What?"

"Oh, yeah. Don't get me wrong, now. She loved Ronnie like a daughter, but she didn't think she was supposed to be with you forever. Selena, though? She thought y'all were meant to be. Don't know how she came to that conclusion, but that's what she thought. She was real sad when she left."

"Wow. I had no idea," Mordecai said, still surprised at finding out his parents knew about his mistress. For some reason, something told him that Selena was closer to him than he originally thought.

"Where's your wife?"

8

———————

"**N**igga. Move," Siah laughed as he pushed Bryce out of his face. They were celebrating after yet another win, this one against the Giants. They had won by a touchdown, a field goal, and a safety, and everyone was stoked. The season was going even better than the one prior where Siah led them to another Super Bowl victory.

"I'm just sayin', bruh. We six and one and in first place. I'm tryna get me a bad bitch before we fly back home and you trippin'," Bryce said with narrowed eyes at his best friend. Siah could do nothing but cackle at his homeboy because at twenty-eight, he was still as much of a hoe as he was at twenty-one.

"I ain't stopping you, fool. I'm just not goin' with you. Besides, my cousin Moriah and her lil boyfriend came to the game so I'm chillin' with her for a minute."

"Oh, shit. Bad, fine ass Moriah came to the game?"

Siah gave his friend a long look and Bryce just lifted his hands in surrender. Siah still remembered how Bryce flirted with Moriah all those years ago and he didn't need those kinds of problems. Siah shook his head and pushed his friend one more time before slapping hands with Avery and a few of his other teammates. His other teammates were still celebrating when he left the locker room to find Moriah. Shockingly but not surprisingly, he found her standing in the corridor alone.

"What you doin' out here by yourself, Mo?" Siah asked his little cousin who hugged him tight.

"It's just me," she said with a small smile, but he could tell something was bothering her.

"What you mean it's just you? Didn't ole boy come with you?"

"Nope. I came by myself and don't look like that," she told him with a raised brow.

"You know I can't stand that nigga, but Ima let you make it since I'm in a good mood."

"Good mood? You better be in a great mood. Passed for over four hundred yards and a rushing touchdown. Didn't know your old ass still had it in you, cousin," Moriah joked as she grinned her dimpled grin and widened her hazel eyes.

"Old? Girl, I'm only twenty-seven. Don't do that shit," Messiah laughed. They talked for a few more minutes before Avery came to tell him they were headed back to the hotel.

"You got somewhere to be? If not, you can come chill at the hotel for a minute?" Siah asked Moriah who took out her phone and texted someone.

"I'll be right behind you."

On the way to the hotel, Siah had calls and texts to return, but saw he had one from his new friend Sharell. He'd been conversing with her pretty consistently over the last month and he'd grown to really like her vibe. He could tell she was a little conceited, but it wasn't so bad that it was a turn off. Besides that though, she seemed like a cool person and so far, things were looking good between them.

He got settled in some comfortable clothing and went back down to the lobby. They were staying in an upscale hotel where discretion was implied so he luckily didn't have to sneak in the shadows to get from one place to the next.

He saw Moriah sitting in the lobby shaking her head at her phone and knew it was probably about her punk ass boyfriend. He didn't like him much, but off the strength of Moriah, he'd tolerate him until he messed up badly enough to be addressed.

They stayed up and hung out for hours before Moriah took her leave. Siah had a six o'clock flight so he figured he could get a two-hour nap before getting ready to head home. His season was about to start getting challenging and he had to get his head in the game.

Moriah returned to Chicago the next day around noon and her mood was still dismal. She'd had a wonderful weekend in New York with Derrick.

That is, until he had to fly back Sunday morning because of an emergency at work. Why he couldn't handle the emergency on Monday morning upset her and they ended up arguing about it while he packed to leave. She knew he was happy for the excuse to leave since it meant not having to go to the game that afternoon and that made her even more angry.

She cursed him out and let it go. She went to the game and sat in the box like her cousin wanted and enjoyed watching him in action. All in all, her trip was a success. At least it felt like it, until she landed and saw the text messages left by Derrick. He was still in his feelings about her ignoring him the night before, like he hadn't left her in a strange city alone.

"This nigga," she murmured to herself as she sat in the back of her Uber. She tried to relax on the way to her and Senai's apartment. They still lived downtown, but in a more spacious place.

People thought it odd that two grown women that could afford to live separately still decided to room together, but it worked well for them. Plus, Moriah would never admit it aloud, but she didn't like the idea of living alone and she had a feeling that Senai knew that as well.

It was Monday so Senai would be in class and labs all day long and Moriah knew she could get comfortable and pig out on the couch. Before she did that, she took a long shower and went to her room to catch up with her dad.

"Hey, Daddy," Moriah said over the phone as she dressed in her Winnie the Pooh t-shirt gown and put a scarf around her edges.

"Hey, Peanut. You back and settled?"

"Yes sir, I am. I'm about to get comfortable and chill out for the day," she said as she went to the kitchen and grabbed her pineapple chunks and ate them from the container.

They talked for a little while before she ended the call with the promise of her coming to the house to see him later that day. She turned on the Bluetooth speaker and let the music calm her down and closed her eyes to meditate. She hated that she missed church the day before so she'd have to make sure she made bible study on Wednesday. She always felt off if she didn't start her week listening to a preacher that genuinely cared about what he was saying.

She and Senai usually accompanied their grandparents

to their church, but if not, caught the online streaming service from the megachurch that Siah attended in Atlanta. They might not be at service every week, but their family took their spirituality very seriously.

When she had her mind and spirit in a better place, she decided to return Derrick's texts and let him know she'd see him later. For now, she was going to chill, take a nap, and enjoy her alone time.

"Well? Did you get your emergency taken care of?" Moriah asked Derrick as she stood in the doorway of his office. She had to stop herself from licking her lips at her man because he always dressed like a boss when he was at work and that day was no exception.

"I did, actually," Derrick said as he looked away from his computer screen and did a double take to take Moriah in.

When she'd woken from her nap, she felt at ease and wanted to look how she felt. She wore a pair of high waisted acid wash jeans, a low cut top that showed off the beginning of her sternum tattoo, an oversized blazer that was rolled up at the elbow, and a pair of high heeled block heels. She had her hair down with a part down the middle and even though Renee had given her a trim, it still fell to her shoulders.

Just because she wasn't working didn't mean she'd come to her workplace looking any kind of way and with the way Derrick looked like he wanted to lick her from head to toe, she figured she wasn't looking too bad.

"You look," Derrick shook his head and couldn't get his words out. She smiled bashfully and felt her face heat up with a blush she couldn't stop. He got up from his desk and made his way over to her and kissed her lips. Their boss was okay with dating inside the workplace as long as it didn't affect business and since they were in two different departments, it never seemed to cause a problem.

"I'm sorry again for having to leave, honey. I know that was supposed to be our time and work ruined it. I'll make it up to you," Derrick said as he looked at her. He seemed genuine so she smiled and gave him a peck before they were interrupted.

"Oh, I didn't realize you had company," came a voice too close to Moriah for her comfort. She turned and saw a woman who looked to be of mixed ethnicity, maybe Asian and Black, very petite in size and height, and with a dress that seemed overly inappropriate for work.

"And yet, you didn't leave when you realized," Moriah stated calmly when she saw the woman didn't attempt to leave when she saw someone in Derrick's office.

"Moriah," Derrick chastised her before turning back towards the woman. "Haven, this is Moriah Jackson. She's one of the mental health counselors here. Moriah, this is Haven Kakoa, our new accountant."

"Ahhh, *of course* she is," Moriah said as she stood to leave. Haven looked her up and down and Moriah could tell she couldn't find anything wrong from the way she pinched her thin lips together.

"I'll see you later tonight, Der. Be at my house no later than eight," Moriah said as she bent down to pick up her purse.

"Your house? Isn't that inappropriate?" Haven asked snidely. Moriah could already tell she was going to be a problem.

"It probably would be if we weren't together, but seeing as we are, I think it's okay. And let's make that our last time questioning something that has nothing to do with you, yes?" Moriah said as she came to stand in front of Haven with a sweet smile.

"Moriah, stop being rude. Haven, I'll see you in the meeting at three," Derrick said as he stood. Haven smirked slightly at Moriah before walking out and Moriah scoffed softly before turning around to look at him.

"Tell me now," Moriah said, looking at a confused Derrick.

"Tell you what?"

"Don't insult my intelligence, Derrick. Have you fucked, sucked, or promised anything to that woman that wasn't work related? I'm giving you a chance to explain."

"Moriah, what kind of fucked up questioning is that?"

"Apparently, something you can't seem to answer. I know women like her and I know men. If you want your little protégé, you tell me now. Not when I find you on top of her or when she's on her knees in front of you."

"I never took you for the insecure type."

"Oh, baby. The way I have you moaning my name, I have no reason to be. But, some men like having more than they need and I won't accept having a co-pilot. Like I said, tell me now so we can move on."

Derrick walked over to her and held her face in his hands. "Moriah, I promise. There is nothing going on." She was slightly taller because of her heels so she tilted her head down to give him a passionate kiss that had him squeezing her cheeks.

"I'll see you tonight then. Bring some work clothes, too. I'm pretty sure when I'm done with you, you won't have the energy to go anywhere," Moriah smirked when she saw him bricking up in his slacks. She turned to leave and blew him a kiss.

When she left his office, she felt eyes on her and noticed Haven looking from her office that was down the hall. She had a stank face that Moriah winked at before getting on the elevator. She was headed to her dad's for the rest of the evening but she had a feeling what she just went through wasn't over.

"Nothing my ass," she muttered to herself.

"ALL I'M SAYING IS, I think the bitch should be paying me for letting her top me off," Zeus said jokingly. Everyone laughed but Baby shook his head at his boy.

They'd just left the strip club after handling some business and Zeus found a stripper to take to one of the back rooms and got some head, or at least tried to.

"I'm serious, Baby. I mean, damn. How you on my lap talkin' mad shit and can't do nothin'? Hoes ain't made like they used to be," he continued. Baby knew he was serious and could do nothing but laugh at his friend. Apparently, the girl talked a good game, but could barely do anything without gagging and complaining. He finally got his nut after letting her know she could either suck him off right or get one of her friends to do it instead.

Baby responded to his craziness as he fired up his blunt. "You picked her, hell. I thought you knew what she could do."

"Shit, she was fine and her body was made up good so I figured "when in Rome." Never again, though. Shoulda known these Detroit hoes was something else."

Baby, Zeus, and his team, were all in Detroit for a few days. Though he was helping Chi with the drug portion of their empire, his main control was still their guns, women, and gambling. Their gambling and women ran out of

Detroit and guns through St. Louis. He and Zeus were in Detroit to check on the escorting service that was becoming more lucrative by the day.

Their clients ranged from prominent politicians to university presidents. Every man or woman that wanted to become a client had to pay a "finder's fee" after an extensive background check and signing a nondisclosure agreement. Every customer had something to lose and Baby made sure of it. They did have the legal side of their escorting business, for dates and events only, but the real money came in through the prostitution that most of the girls under their care supplied.

After checking in with his parents, Baby sent texts to Siah, Chi, Senai, and Moriah to let them know he was safe and would be back the next day. He and his crew went their separate ways while Baby and Zeus had one more stop before retiring for the night.

"He let me know he's inside so I guess we can walk up," Baby said as he parked the black Escalade on the street in front of the family home. They checked their surroundings and knocked on the door and waited for it to open.

"Damn, Tre. Took you long enough."

"Shut up, nigga. I had to make sure my baby was good. Hurry up, you lettin' all the heat out," Tre told Zeus as he dapped him and Baby up.

"Shut yo young old ass up. *You lettin' all the heat out.* We need to get you back to the Chi 'cause clearly being in Detroit making you soft," Zeus joked. Tre just sucked his teeth and ignored him and started to chop it up with Baby about what he'd seen and heard in the streets concerning them.

All those years ago when Mouse, Drique, Terrance, and Tre stole money and product from the Jacksons, Chi and

Baby were furious. They treated their workers with respect and made sure they paid them well enough to not try to do something shady like steal, but they got greedy and did so anyway.

Mouse was easy to handle and Micah and Mordecai got Terrance without anyone knowing, sending him to prison on federal charges, but finding Drique and Tre a state away took longer than they wanted. When they found them, they immediately saw how remorseful Tre was and after hearing his reason for stealing, which was to help his mother pay for his little sister's surgery, Baby felt a connection to the young man and convinced Chi that he could still be useful to them.

They killed Drique without a second thought and Tre was shot twice in the chest. Baby strategically placed the bullets so they'd cause a tremendous amount of pain and could have killed him if they didn't get him assistance, but they had a doctor on call waiting for him. They had their foot soldiers leave after they witnessed both shootings and knew they'd spread the word.

Tre was privately hospitalized under a pseudonym and nursed back to health. When he was better, they gave him the option of leaving forever or continuing to work for them but as a ghost that got information and people when needed.

He was loyal and chose to stay with the empire with Isaiah taking him under his wing and helping him with whatever he needed. He moved to Detroit with his mother and sister and had been there ever since and even had a girlfriend and a six-month-old baby girl.

"It's a dude talkin' mad shit about the girls 'cause he can't get in. Talkin' about he's gonna call the laws in to get it shut down," Tre said as he looked back and forth between Baby and Zeus.

"Set up a meeting. I wanna see who this nigga is before we handle it," Baby said. Even though the law was on their side in Chicago as well as Detroit, they hated getting extra attention, especially with Chi hopefully getting out of prison sooner on good behavior.

They spoke for an hour more about what needed to happen the next morning and left. Baby got to his hotel suite and showered and prayed before getting in bed. Sometimes, he wished he had a woman to be with after a long day, but he couldn't rush it. Until then, he'd just enjoy his time being a boss.

9

———————

KIARA

"**S**o he's really acting like this girl ain't constantly disrespecting you?" Kiara asked Moriah who sat beside her with a tall glass of wine.

Kiara, Andrea, Senai, and Moriah were together for their biweekly girls' night at her home and Moriah was filling them in on the craziness that had been going on for the last month and a half in her life.

"Sis, yes. And when I bring up the fact that the heifer is always being slick with her mouth, he says that I'm imagining things. I'm not stupid and I know her little ass wants him," Moriah said with a hard eye roll and gulped down her wine.

"What you gon' do? I mean, does it seem like they're doing something or what?" Andrea asked as she fixed a plate for herself.

"I don't think they are but I don't know what they're doing while they're supposedly working since they're on a different floor than me. It's just like he's not taking me seriously. He knows how I feel about it, but he's either laughing it off or ignoring it altogether. I'm not about to fight over dick that I don't own though, that's for sure."

"That you don't own?" Senai's light voice asked through a chuckle.

"Yes, Nai! I won't fight over dick that I'm not married to. When that happens, I'm killing these hoes on sight," Moriah said confidently while the rest of them laughed.

"I know that's right, boo," Kiara said as she cackled at her sister-in-law. She hadn't had a problem with women coming to her about Chi since high school, besides the one he'd cheated on her with all those years ago, but if one did, it wouldn't be any talking involved. She could guarantee that.

"You need to sit down and have a serious talk with him, Riah," Senai told her. Andrea pursed her lips and Kiara groaned because they all knew Senai hated violence and confrontation, but they felt talking wouldn't help the situation.

"Now wait, y'all. When I say talk, it's a process," Senai proceeded before setting her wine down on the table. She sat up on the chaise she was lying on and continued. "You need to sex him so good he's incoherent. I mean, go in your freak porn star bag and do some things you've never done before and when he's on the brink of consciousness, you scare the hell out of him."

By the time she finished, Kiara, Andrea, and Moriah were all paying close attention to their soft spoken friend. She was putting ideas out that they'd never thought of. Kiara was impressed and intrigued at her little sister who she'd known more than half of her life. She didn't know she had it in her.

"You always say he's a little wary being around Mecca and Siah, but Riah, you're a Jackson, too and I think he might have forgotten that. When he's almost asleep, you get on top of him with a blade to his throat and let him know you're not the one to play with.

"I think by the time you finish your talk, he'll understand the severity of the situation," Senai finished, picking up her wine glass and sipping it like she hadn't just told someone to threaten their significant other.

"Shit, bitch! You need to stop hanging with Baby and Zeus 'cause got damn!" Andrea yelled out after they were all quiet for a few moments. They were shocked but Moriah knew Senai better and didn't seem to be as shaken up as Kiara and Andrea.

Kiara thought she was a savage but the way Senai spoke had her thinking that her little sister had her beat. Senai's crazy reminded her of Siah's and she could do nothing but shake her head at that.

They laughed and continued with their night and talked about their relationships and work and whatever else came to mind. Kiara checked her cell and saw a message from her mother about Mercy wanting her to call her before she went to bed, so Kiara stepped away from her girls and went to the spare bedroom and dialed her mom.

"Hey, lovey. How's girls' night going?" Kam asked. She always kept Mercy when they did their night. Even though they rarely went out for their time together, Kam liked having her own girls' night with her grandbaby and it was the perfect time to do so.

"It's good, Mama. Where's Ci-Ci?"

"She just ran off somewhere, girl. We already did our nails and facials so I think she went to go pick a Disney movie to watch."

"Of course she did. I don't know why since we all know she'll be asleep in an hour," Kiara laughed softly at her baby.

She was spoiled rotten and loved having her spa days but afterwards, was always so relaxed she'd fall asleep. To be almost four, she was on a set bedtime and fell asleep like clockwork.

"Aw, leave my baby alone. Oh, here she is. Hold on," Kam said before passing the phone to Mercy.

"Mommy! Hi, Mommy," Mercy said excitedly.

"Hey, mama. How's your night going so far, Ci-Ci?"

"It's good, Mommy. Grandma painted my toes light pink and I got a fasal, Mommy." Kiara laughed lightly at Mercy mispronouncing facial. She could speak really well to be so young, but she still had problems with certain words.

"It's called a facial, baby. But, I'm glad you're having fun. You talked to Daddy, tonight?"

"Uh huh! He called Grandma and we talked for a long time. He said he has a surprise for me."

Kiara rolled her eyes. Chi loved telling her he had a surprise when he knew she didn't need anything else in her room. Mercy wasn't bratty, thankfully, but if her dad kept buying her unnecessary toys and gifts, she might get that way.

"That's good, baby. We'll have to see what it is. I know you're about to watch a movie and get ready for bed so I'm gonna let you go, okay?"

"Okay, Mommy. See you tomorrow. Love you!"

"Love you more, mama. I'll see you in the morning."

A FEW DAYS LATER, Kiara was able to leave work early and decided to stop by her mother's house before picking Mercy up from daycare. Renee was manning the salon for the day because Kam wasn't feeling her best.

Kiara wanted to check on her and make sure she didn't need anything. She lived in a nice gated community and once Kiara put in the code to get into the gate, she slowly drove to her mother's home, but stopped short when she saw a familiar vehicle in the driveway.

"No, no, no. Maybe it's just a friendly visit," Kiara told herself once she parked in the street. She got out of her car and was walking slowly towards the front door when it opened and she saw her mother stand on her tiptoes and kiss him on the lips.

"Seriously?" Kiara called out and surprised them both.

"Kiara! What are you doing here, lovey?" Kam nervously asked her while looking back and forth between them both, him still not having said a word.

"How long has this been going on?" Kiara asked, but was looking at him.

"KiKi—"

"Uh uh. I know you and I know you're about to give me an excuse and I don't want it. I just wanna know how long you two been messing around," Kiara said to him.

"We aren't messing around, KiKi. We've been together for about a year and a half," he said before grabbing Kam's hand and pulling her out of the house.

"Lovey. Say something," Kam said to Kiara who had been standing there for a minute without speaking a word.

"I don't even know what to say. I mean—so...you two are serious?" Kiara stuttered, asking them both to which her mother looked up at him and he smiled down at her and she looked back at Kiara and nodded.

"How about we go back inside and we talk about it," he suggested. Kiara nodded hesitantly after a moment and her mother grabbed her hand and brought her inside and sat her on the loveseat beside her while he sat in the chair across from them. When they were settled, Kam grabbed Kiara's hands again and smiled softly at her.

"You know I had you young at seventeen. Your father promised me a lot of things and your grandparents were so strict and traditional that I rebelled and I just ignored all the red flags and listened to him. He got me pregnant and basically disappeared.

"Being the African parents they were, your grandparents kicked me out because I wasn't living up to their expectations and luckily, your aunt had an apartment already so I lived with her until I graduated high school and I moved here. I got into college and I worked hard to make a life for you. I lucked up and met Renee when you were ten and the rest is history," Kam paused and looked at him who nodded his head.

"When you were about fourteen, I came across your father again and I told him about you. He still didn't want anything to do with you, but his wife, that angel, she wanted to meet you. You remember you met her first," Kam said and Kiara nodded. She met Lisa secretly for about three years before she met her father.

"Anyway, Lisa got me in touch with Reggie and he helped a lot as far as finances and whatever you needed, and Lisa did too, but she couldn't do as much. Fast forward ten years and you have Mercy and it's like your dad suddenly wants to be around. He starts calling me to get you to see him so he can be around her and well, you know what happened."

"Where do you come in then, Uncle?" Kiara turned towards him.

"I met your mother when you were maybe twelve the first time. At the time, I didn't know she had my niece. Two years later, we met again, but through Lisa this time. She didn't need any help, but she had you and I knew my ain't shit brother wasn't pulling his weight so I stepped in. We've been close for years, but when Mercy came, I don't know. We became inseparable because she loves being with us at one time. One thing led to another and we've been together officially for a year or so."

Kiara tried to take in all the information given to her. Her mother and her father's brother were in a secret relationship. She didn't disagree with the union because honestly, Reggie was like a father to her anyway and she had noticed the happy change in her mother, but figured she had started back casually dating. Kam had trust issues like crazy because of what her father did to her and seeing how she'd been in a serious relationship all this time made her happy for her. She just didn't know it would be with her uncle.

"Does my dad know?" Kiara asked them.

"Not yet, but he will," Reggie said.

"Reg—"

"No, Kammy, he needs to know. I'm tired of staying in the shadows just to keep the peace. You're my woman and the world deserves to know," Reggie said as he looked at Kam whose dark skin looked a little more rosy than usual. Kiara couldn't help but to smile at them.

"So, it was my mom you were with a few months ago that had you missing that Sunday dinner, huh?" Kiara asked her uncle with a smirk. He looked confused for a second before coughing out a laugh.

"Yeah, she's the reason. She needed some supplies for the shop and we went to go get them and I was late coming back."

"Okay. I like this. I'm glad you're happy," Kiara said softly with a nod as she turned towards her mother who released a breath and let her eyes get glossy. She hugged her tightly before kissing her cheek. She checked her watch and saw she had to leave to get her daughter so she said her good-byes and left the house with a smile on her face.

"Who'd a thunk it?" Kiara asked herself as she drove to get Mercy.

10

———————

SIAH

"You serious?" Siah asked her as he looked over at her.

"Yes, Messiah. I told you I don't feel comfortable doing that. It just feels wrong," Sharell said looking at Siah with her nose turned up.

Siah rubbed down his waves to keep himself calm. He was a grown ass man and was really with a woman that didn't feel comfortable going down on him. He never thought he'd be here.

He really did like Sharell, but it was hang ups like that that had him second guessing himself. It wasn't the fact that he *needed* it per se, but it was different when it wasn't even an option.

He had decided to take their relationship to the next level after going to his fourth Super Bowl two months before. She had been there when his team didn't come out victorious and their relationship grew tremendously. At least, certain aspects had grown.

"You feel the same way when I'm giving you head or is it just when you do it?"

"No, I really like when you do it and I don't see a problem when you do. I just feel it's degrading for a lady. It makes me feel like a hoe," Sharell said with a shrug.

Siah squinted his eyes at her and tried to calm his heart. He didn't understand her thinking and he didn't know if he wanted to think about it. She thought a lot of things were beneath her and unladylike. She came from an upper middle class family, similar to his own mother, but unlike his mother, she was conceited to the umpteenth degree—much more than he originally thought.

She didn't give head, didn't think certain sexual positions and activities were that of a respectable woman, and only wanted to do certain activities for their dates. She didn't do outdoor things, like biking or hiking or even long walks because she didn't like to sweat that much. She did do yoga and pilates but that's about it. Siah did have some effect on her though because she was open to do a little more than she used to, so hopefully he could get her out of her other close-minded ways.

Just when he was about to respond to her, his phone rang. He looked down and his brows rose in intrigue when he saw who was calling. He told Sharell he'd be right back and answered the call as he stepped outside.

"Didn't think I'd hear from you today," Siah answered with a smile.

"Ha. Ha. Real funny. Hi, Messi," Senai answered with her light voice. He could tell she had a smile on her face.

"To what do I owe the pleasure, Miss Williamson?"

"I'm here and wanted to see if you were busy," Senai answered hesitantly. Siah looked at his phone and thought for a second before answering.

"You're here? Like in Atlanta?"

"Yeah. I had to come for a conference. We made it in this

morning and we have a free night to explore the city or whatever before we start tomorrow and I thought...well, since you're here, I thought I'd ask if you wanted to do something," Senai said.

"You don't have to, of course. I'm sure you have plans and stuff. That was stupid of me to just ask for you to make time for me without warning," Senai babbled on when Siah didn't say anything. He finally zoned back in to Senai apologizing and hurriedly interrupted.

"Naiya! It's cool. I was just surprised, that's all. We can definitely go out, for sure. I know you don't like a lot of attention so we can go to my homegirl's spot? She can cook literally anything. She'd love to meet you, I'm sure," Siah said.

LaShea had met his parents and Baby in the few years he'd known her, but not the entire family. She definitely knew who Senai was and would be ecstatic about meeting her.

"Yes, that would be great! I don't wanna be an inconvenience, though. I can reimburse her for anything she buys for the evening if that'll help?" Senai asked which made Siah smile at his Bratz doll. Even when nervous, her manners always came through.

"Naiya, shut up. You know better than that," Siah told her and heard her whisper an apology and he couldn't help feel himself grow in sweats. Senai was so naturally submissive it was ridiculous, but he loved that about her.

They talked for a few minutes more before agreeing that Siah would pick her up from her hotel at eight o'clock and they'd head to LaShea's apartment. He headed back inside with a smile that had his dimple and a half standing out and Sharell looked at him with an attitude.

"What's with you?" she asked.

"Shit. Going to Shea's, though," he answered looking down at his phone so he could text her to let her know she had to cook for them.

He caught Sharell rolling her eyes before she turned away from him. He knew Sharell wasn't a fan of LaShea's since she found out she used to strip. Another one of the things that Sharell found beneath her. She knew better than to express her aversion to LaShea's job choices because LaShea would probably hurt her feelings. Plus, Sharell's bark was bigger than her bite so she only talked a good game.

"Thought you were chilling with me tonight? Change your mind?" she asked with an attitude.

"Nope, but I will be back here later than originally planned," Siah responded as he stretched and grabbed his keys to leave.

"Why you goin' over there tonight out of all nights?" she asked him with her hands on her wide hips.

He turned to look at her and saw she was headed into a mood. Her slanted eyes that were done up with glittery eyeshadow that made her skin tone glow a radiant brown were narrowed at him. Her button nose was wrinkled in frustration and her thick lips covered in lip gloss were scrunched in aggravation.

Even with her face turned up, he couldn't deny she was beautiful. He walked over to her slowly and tilted her head up by her chin. She pouted at him and he kissed her lips.

"A family friend is in town and she wants to hang out before she gets to work tomorrow. She's not really a people person so I'm taking her to Shea's," he told her and she scoffed and rolled her eyes.

"A family friend? Really?" she asked.

"That's what I said. You know I don't like to repeat myself," Siah said firmly and she rolled her eyes again.

"Fine. I guess I will see you here when you're done then," Sharell said after looking at him for a few seconds. He didn't say anything but nodded his head and kissed her forehead before letting himself out.

"There's Miss Naiya. I was wondering when you'd show your face," Siah called out to Senai when he spotted her coming through the hotel lobby doors.

He was leaning on the passenger side of his Range Rover and had to hold in a grin as he watched her come out of the hotel dressed in tights and a hoodie. Even though the hoodie wasn't fitted, it still couldn't hide the hips that swayed side to side as she walked near him with a nervous smile.

"Hey, Messi. Thanks again for picking me up," Senai told Siah before she leaned in and gave him a hug that made him want to hold her tighter, but pulled away only a few seconds into the hug after inhaling the fruity aroma of her hair.

"Come on. I'm about to show you how these southern folks get down," Siah told her as he opened the passenger door for her.

They caught up as he drove them to LaShea's house. She let him know she was in town for four days to network and see where she could see herself next.

"I wanna leave Chicago, I think, but I'm not sure. It's so hard to decide," Senai confided in him.

"You know what I told you when you first started on this journey. You have to decide for you and no one else. You're gonna shine wherever you go, Naiya. Just make sure you're happy while you're shining," Siah said seriously. He could tell she was thinking about what he said but gave him a small nod in return.

He pulled into the parking spot in front of LaShea's place and looked over at Senai who was wringing her hands. He smiled softly at her profile because Senai was always nervous to meet new people, but she was so likable that she had no reason to be.

"So, this is my girl Shea's place. She's actually a year younger than you so y'all might have a lot in common. She's real cool though so I know y'all will get along. Her man, Avery, is a teammate of mine and he's a jokester but he's good people, too. You ready?" he asked her. He saw her take in a big breath before slowly exhaling.

"Ready."

11

SENAI

Senai claimed to be ready, but when Siah came to her side to walk her to the door, she was shaking on the inside. She always felt weird meeting new people, but meeting someone close to Siah was different. She didn't understand why, but it just felt like...more.

"Finally! Why I thought you'd actually be here on time I'll never understand," Senai heard a feminine voice fuss. When she came into view, Senai had to stop herself from dropping her jaw because she was truly a beautiful young woman. For some reason, Senai couldn't stop herself from staring at her because she seemed familiar to her but she couldn't put her finger on why.

"Oh my gosh! You really do look like a doll. I thought he was exaggerating. I'm LaShea, but you can call me Shea if you want," LaShea said as she went to hug Senai. Senai liked her right away and hugged her tightly.

"It's nice to meet you. I'm guessing you already know, but my name is Senai. And thank you again for letting me come over. I'm not really into crowds," Senai said as she came further into the townhome with Siah not far behind.

"No, thank you. I haven't met all of Siah's folks so meeting you feels like I'm really one of the family. Plus, I don't really have a lot of girl friends so it's nice to hang out with someone I get along with, even if it is just for a night," LaShea told Senai who couldn't help but smile at her genuineness.

"Aight, aight. Calm all that down and come on so we can eat," Siah said loudly, breaking up their moment. LaShea made a silly face mockingly while Senai giggled lowly.

Avery came from the kitchen with the food in hand and set it on the dining room table before turning to speak to Siah and introduce himself to Senai. He was handsome with his smooth, dark skin and locs that were long and braided neatly into two braids. He had laugh lines on his face that appeared when he spoke with a sharp jawline and dark brown eyes that were kind and inviting. He had to be around the same height as Siah, but was much leaner, as a wide receiver normally was. He was playful like Siah said he would be and Senai couldn't stop the smiles and the laughs that spilled from her lips.

LaShea had prepared fried catfish and spaghetti for their meal and Senai hadn't had the two together since she was a kid, but loved it once she tried it again. The night was definitely a success and she couldn't help but to love the fact that she was enjoying the night with Siah by her side.

When they were getting ready to leave, Senai hugged her new friends and found herself looking at LaShea again. She'd caught herself doing it throughout the night, but it was like she couldn't help herself. She really did feel like she reminded her of someone.

"I can't wait to see you again. If you ever need a getaway, please don't hesitate to call me. I'm done with school, so I'm ready whenever," LaShea grinned at her and that's when it came to her.

"I got it! You look like my best friend," Senai called out, proud of herself for finally figuring it out. When she said it, LaShea looked at Siah for confirmation and even he looked closely, as if he was seeing her for the first time.

"I can see it, actually. You're not nearly as light as she is and her hazel eyes are mostly green, but yeah, you do look like her," Siah mumbled with a weird look on his face.

"Well if I look like *that* modelesque stallion, I gotta be doing something right," LaShea joked. Avery must have whispered something nasty to her because she blushed before pushing him back and telling them goodbye, followed by Avery, who said he'd hook Senai up with some tickets for the next season which had her excited.

"That was so much fun! Thank you, Messi," Senai beamed as they rode down the highway.

"You're welcome, Naiya. Glad you enjoyed yourself," Siah answered after chuckling at her enthusiasm. She normally would feel embarrassed, but she couldn't at the moment. She rarely allowed herself time to just be, especially because of her class and lab schedule, so besides her girls' nights, she didn't get out much.

"So, how is Grandma Althea? You know that's my baby," Siah asked with a small smirk on his handsome face. He looked over to Senai and she almost combusted right there. She subtly squeezed her thighs together before clearing her throat to answer him.

"She's good. You know her, always on the go and with Grandma Emma. I think she's seeing one of the deacons at the church, but I can't prove it," Senai replied as she glanced at him.

"Deacon Wright?"

"How'd you know?"

"'Cause he's the only one that can handle her. I mean she's what? Sixty-five or so? And she still fine as hell. She couldn't be with an older man that acts like an old man. I mean yo grandaddy was healthy as an ox and died in an accident, not anything health related," Siah responded and looked at Senai's straight face and cackled loudly.

"That's disgusting."

"I don't see the problem. At least we know what you'll look like later in life," Siah said with a shrug of his shoulder as he turned into the hotel parking lot.

Senai could do nothing but blush at his bluntness. She had been hearing that she looked like her grandmother all of her life so she was used to it, but it was different when Siah said it.

"Alright, Naiya Baby. If you have some time away from your conference, hit me up. We can do lunch or something," Siah said as he parked in front of the hotel and turned towards her.

"That sounds nice. I'll definitely let you know," Senai said, smiling shyly. Siah stared at her for a few moments and Senai's face heated at his gaze, but she didn't look away from his hazel eyes.

"What?" she asked softly. Siah huffed out a laugh before a small smile graced his face.

"Nothing. Go on up and get to bed. You got a long day ahead of you," he uttered quietly without taking his eyes off of her.

"Yeah, guess you're right. Thanks again," Senai said before leaning over and kissing Siah's cheek and saying a quick goodnight.

She hurriedly left his vehicle and walked towards the

entrance, but turned just in time to see Siah shaking his head as he drove away.

She couldn't keep the smile off of her face until she fell asleep not even half an hour later.

SENAI ROLLED her luggage through O'Hare looking for her ride when she heard her name hollered from across the airport. She looked around and saw Moriah standing there waving her hands like she hadn't seen her in months instead of just a few days.

She had already expressed how much she missed Senai and had been staying with both her dad and with Derrick because she hated staying home alone at night. When she made it to her, Moriah basically tackled her and she could do nothing but laugh.

"I've got amazing news! I didn't wanna tell it to you over the phone so I had to wait until you got here," Moriah grinned with her hazel eyes bright and smiling.

"Uhh, well spring it on me. It has to be really good for you to be acting like this," Senai said as they walked to Moriah's Jeep. They buckled up and Moriah took off down the highway.

"He's coming home, Nai. He's actually coming home," Moriah said as she got choked up. Senai was so shocked that she was speechless for a minute, before she shrieked loudly.

"Are you serious? When? How? I just-oh my God!" Senai said, struggling to come up with words to articulate exactly how she felt.

"I know! Apparently, our lawyers found out how dirty the police department was because the search warrant they had first wasn't even signed. The one they presented in court was a fake."

"Are you freaking kidding me? How did they just now find out, though?"

"The captain that gave them the okay to do the bust just retired so they were able to go in and talk to some of the narcs and got them to fess up. They've done it to a whole lot of people before my brother. My daddy already said we're suing the hell out of the department when Chi gets out."

"Oh my gosh, that's amazing. How's Kiara taking the news? I just know she's over the moon."

"She actually doesn't know," Moriah said slowly.

"Why not?"

"Chi wants to surprise her. He's gonna act like everything is normal and then just pop up whenever he gets out," Moriah said as she shrugged with a smile on her face.

"That's so sweet," Senai exclaimed. She couldn't believe the news but was even more excited for Kiara and little Mercy.

"I know right. We're not sure of the exact date but it should be around summertime."

"This is just," Senai couldn't even finish her sentence but shook her head in awe. She said a quick prayer of thanks and continued catching up with Moriah who was just as excited for her spending time with her cousin.

"Soooo. Impromptu double date with Messiah, huh?" Moriah teased.

"Shut up. It wasn't a date," Senai said with a huff, but was blushing hard.

"Oh? Did you not say it was just you, Si, his friend, and her man? Hmmm. Two pairs of people? Check. Food? Check. Underlying sexual tension? Double check," Moriah answered smartly with a coy dimpled smile as she turned on Althea's street.

"Forget you. He was just helping me out."

"If that's the case, why didn't he invite his lil girlfriend?"

"I—"

"Exactly. He left her ass at home so he could come and be with who he actually wants to be with, if only until midnight. You're like Cinderella, the homewrecker edition," Moriah said before laughing loudly at the offended look on Senai's face.

"I think it's nice that you went out with him without any of us there. When y'all finally do get the balls to be together, maybe that'll be the moment you look back on as the catalyst," Moriah told her friend as she pulled up to Althea's home.

"Whatever. We both know that isn't happening," Senai responded somberly.

"Anyway, thanks for dropping me off. I'll be home later on," Senai said before blowing her a kiss and heading inside her grandmother's house. Before she could get in the door, she looked at the street and saw a luxury vehicle and was eager to get inside.

"I knew that was you!" Senai yelled out when she saw her uncle Jonathan sitting in the living room.

"I told you I was making a trip soon," Jonathan told her as he stood and brought her in for a tight embrace. She hadn't seen him in a couple of months even though they spoke often.

"You know Jamaal keeps me busy and with Tonya pregnant again, it's hard to move like I want. But, I'm here," he continued. Soon after Jean's father died, Jonathan conveniently divorced her. He met his current girlfriend Tonya three years ago and it was a match made in heaven. She got pregnant right away with a little boy they named Jamaal, after Senai's father, and was currently pregnant with a little girl.

Tonya was the complete opposite of Jean and Senai adored her. Even better, Althea did, too. She was a principal at one of the academies in Detroit and at thirty-eight, a few years younger than Jonathan, she still looked years younger. Her tawny skin was always flawless and she was thick, plus sized with amazing curves and was the epitome of full figured.

"Did you at least bring my little monster with you?" Senai asked about her two-year-old cousin Jamaal. He was extremely active and even though he wasn't bad, he didn't sit still and was always into something.

"Yeah, his hyper ass is in the kitchen with Mama. I actually need you to watch him for a little while if you can. I wanted to take her out for an early dinner."

"Sure! I don't have anything to do for the rest of the day," Senai called out as she walked to the kitchen to find Althea and Jamaal at the table coloring.

"Nai Nai! Hi!" Jamaal waved and smiled before going back to his coloring.

"Hey, little monster," Senai said as she kissed the top of his head and leaned over and kissed her grandmother on the cheek. She peeked into the refrigerator and smiled widely when she saw Tupperware containers of food.

"Jay, you're gonna stay here with Senai while Grandma and I go out for a little while, okay?" Jonathan said when he walked into the kitchen.

"Otay, Daddy," he answered without looking up. Senai could do nothing but laugh. Tonya informed her how serious he took his art and was probably the only thing that could get all of his attention for long periods of time.

A couple of hours later, Senai cuddled up under her favorite blanket and was watching tv with her baby cousin beside her. He was on her tablet and had somehow navigated to the internet to an animated show that had his attention so she let him be. She peered down at him as she checked her phone, going back and forth with Baby about how they were going to spend the upcoming weekend.

She saw when Moriah finally responded in their group chat and laughed at the two cousins arguing like only they could and relaxed on the couch and pulled little Jamaal closer to her. He loved to cuddle so he climbed into her lap and went back to his show. She smiled before kissing the top of his head.

Everything seemed right in her life at the moment until she realized she hadn't spoken to Warren. Even worse, she hadn't really thought of him in a day or two. Even more concerning, she didn't feel bad about either of those things and that in itself had her worried.

12

CHI

"Ah, shit. Wait, wait," Kiara pleaded and tried putting her hand behind her back to slow down his movements, but Chi wasn't having that and grabbed her arm and held it instead.

"No can do, Ari. You kept my pussy away from me last week, so now I get to have her how I want," Chi responded calmly as if he wasn't trying to split her in two.

"You act like I could help when my period came. Ahhhhh, baby, hold up. Shit," Kiara whimpered out as he pressed her into the wall with so much force he could tell she was losing her breath. He knew he wasn't hurting her but didn't need her passing out from the pleasure, which she'd done before, so he eased his thrusts a bit.

She was lucky that he only wanted a quickie that day or he'd probably have her against the table and sitting in the chair after, but the way her walls were squeezing him, he couldn't hold out and grunted and groaned out his release. He had to hold her steady as he slowly pulled out of her and kissed her neck when she leaned her body into him to keep her balance.

"Damn, bae. I gotta hurry up and get outta here. You can't even take dick how you used to. Let me find out you a bitch now," Chi joked as he gently hugged her from behind and kissed her neck again.

Before they started messing around in high school, Chi always said he'd only be serious with someone that could take him without complaint. Because Kiara crushed on him so hard, she told him he should give her a chance.

He asked if she really thought she could handle all of him after showing her what he was packing, to which she responded "my mama didn't raise no bitch." It had been a running joke in their relationship for years, and Chi definitely only meant it as a joke because his wife *definitely* could handle him.

"Oh, please. You and I both know I'll have you in that chair moaning like a little girl if we had the time," Kiara said with a raised eyebrow as she turned to look at him. He could do nothing but raise his hands in surrender because she undoubtedly would.

After cleaning themselves up, they sat down at the table in the middle of the room and caught up. It had only been a couple of days since he'd seen her last and only a few hours since they'd spoken, but it always felt like forever since they couldn't see each other everyday. If it was up to Chi, he'd never be away from her.

"I miss you so much, Mal," Kiara said with teary eyes. Her expression concerned Chi so he walked to her side of the table before squatting in front of her. He was so tall, they were about the same height so he was able to look into her eyes to find out what was bothering her.

"Hey, come on, now," he called gently after he saw tears fall. "What's wrong? Talk to me and tell me what's goin' on."

"It's nothing. I just get emotional sometimes and today is the day, I guess."

"I'm so so sorry for this, bae. This is my fault and I swear on Ci-Ci's life that this will never happen again."

"This isn't your fault, Mal."

"Yes, it is. Whether someone put me here or not, I'm the one that put us in this position, but Ari? Bear with me just a little while longer, okay? Whether it be two days, two months, or two years, I'm going to make it better. I swear."

Kiara stared at him with glossy eyes and he felt his chest tighten. He never wanted this for her, but he was too selfish to let her go. He knew it was taxing on her to be without him, especially with a busy-bodied youngster at home, but thankfully, he'd be back home to her in a few months' time. He just hoped she could hold out until then.

"We are going to be okay. Whenever I get out, we're going on a vacation. We're going to renew our vows and then I'm gonna put two or three more Jacksons in you," Chi said while Kiara huffed out a laugh. He smiled softly at her and wiped her face with the pads of his thumbs and kissed her nose. Kiara grabbed both of his hands with hers and smiled.

"I love you, Malachi Vaughn. I know we'll be fine, baby."

"Oh, glad you know 'cause yo fine chocolate ass wasn't goin' nowhere anyway," Chi shrugged and Kiara smacked her lips and pushed him off of her.

The couple conversed and laughed with one another until a guard knocked on the door letting him know it was time. They may have been limited in time together now, but soon, no one would be able to tell him a thing.

∼

"SCOTTIE, man, tell me you got something for me," Chi said as he sat down and looked across the table at his attorney.

"Actually, I do have some good news. The eighteenth of June."

"What you talking," Chi started to ask, but stopped when it came to him. "You serious? Don't play with me right now, Scott."

"I'm serious. I got it set. The judge is getting the paperwork together as we speak and your release date will be next month on the eighteenth," Scottie spoke proudly.

Chi was speechless. When he first found out about the forged warrant, he knew it would be a matter of time before he was out and back to his old life. Scottie and his team told him it would probably be months, maybe late July or early August before he could be released, but to hear that he'd be getting out in roughly five weeks almost made him sob tears of joy.

"Scottie, I don't even know what to say," Chi said, getting choked up. He was never one of those men that was afraid to let his emotions show; he just had so many he didn't know which to let out first.

"You don't have to say a thing. My family has been with you and your people damn near as long you and I been alive. Hell, you're like family to me. We weren't going to stop until we got you out of here," Scottie said emotionally.

Scott Archibald III, or Scottie, was two years older than Chi, but had basically grown up with the Jackson kids. Law was in his blood and with his parents and uncles representing the Jacksons since the nineties, the families were extremely close.

His younger brother was an attorney as well but was focused strictly in divorce and their younger sister was finishing law school but wanted to practice family law. On top of being his lawyer, Scottie also bought a lot of weed from Chi so they were close either way.

"Before you get out, I wanna work on the lawsuit with the department. We can get that underway beforehand so that'll be one less thing to worry about by the time you leave," Scottie continued. Chi nodded his agreement but his mind was already drifting back to the news he'd just received.

Scottie must have also realized it because he laughed and said he'd call him later that week if he had any more updates or news to share. They said their goodbyes and Chi made it back to his cell, full of butterflies and nervous energy. He fell into his barely there mattress and couldn't help the smile that covered his face and felt the tears fall to his ears.

"Thank you, God," he whispered as he shut his eyes and wept.

13

MORDECAI

"Damn shame my own mama been ducking and dodging her eldest child," Mordecai called out into the early morning air as he looked at his mother step outside her front door onto the porch. He must have frightened her because she clutched her chest in surprise.

"Mordecai! Hey, baby," Emma uttered nervously. She tried to force a smile, but he could tell she was avoiding his eyes.

"Been tryna get up with you for like a month now, Emma Lee Jackson, and you been ducking me. I wanna know why."

"Just because you look like your daddy doesn't mean you are him. Talk to me like you got some sense," she chastised softly but firmly and he nodded in apology. "Your daddy told me what you wanted and I thought if I gave you some time, you'd let it go."

"And why would I let it go, Mama? I've been trying to find her for years," Mordecai said as he walked closer to her.

She looked up at him and he couldn't help but to look over his mother. She was radiant at her age and was still in amazing shape thanks to her husband, who made sure his entire family stayed in shape and ate halfway decently. Even at six in the morning, she dressed to impress and she always had her graying hair in a perfectly cut bob that made her light brown skin shine in the sun.

She was only five-foot-four at the most so she always had to look up to the men in her life, but her personality was so big that it made up the difference.

"Come on, Eloi. I guess I owe you the other half of your love story," she sighed as she dragged him down to sit in the rocking chair beside hers. She let out a deep breath like she'd been holding it in for years and started speaking as if she were reading out of a book.

"You don't have to leave, you know? He'll change his mind and you two will be back like you never left," Emma said as she stared at Selena's crestfallen face.

"I don't think so, Ms. Emma. You didn't see how he looked at me when he said it. I think it'll be best if I just leave."

"And what if you change your mind? What if he changes his mind?"

"Then-then God will bring us back together. One way or another," Selena said softly, as if she was trying to convince Emma and herself.

Emma looked at Selena and knew why her son wanted her so badly. She was beautiful, a close look alike to the actress Paula Patton. Besides the physical though, Selena was pure at heart. She was gentle, almost docile, and probably couldn't hurt a fly.

Mordecai had to see her as someone he needed to protect. Someone to watch after carefully. He never had to look at Veronica that way because she was so independent, but this one? This one was Lois Lane and needed her Superman.

Emma loved Veronica, always had. But she also knew she wasn't the one for her son. Her sons were alpha men who needed women who were strong as well, but didn't mind being led, and sadly, Veronica wasn't that.

Nothing was wrong with strong-willed women that didn't want to submit, but there was something wrong with a woman that didn't want to compromise leadership from time to time and Veronica never did. With the business the men were a part of, a united front was needed, but all they did was argue over who was right and who needed to take the blame and that wasn't meant to last.

"You know, when Mordecai was about ten and Micah was around seven, Mordecai had a huge collection of Archie comics. He loved those things and kept them in pristine condition. Well, Micah was an asshole even back then and knew how much his brother loved his comics so one day when he got home earlier than his brother, he went to his room, took one of the comics, and drew in it. Every single page," Emma said with a shake of her head.

"Oh no! What did Mordecai do?" Selena asked, entranced by the story.

"Micah left it out so he could see his handy work and when he came home and saw it, he didn't do a thing. He was quiet and withdrawn for a few days and after talking to his daddy, he stopped being so antisocial, but he still didn't speak to Micah. My baby was more hurt than angry so instead of hitting his brother like his father wanted him to, just so he could be over it, he basically acted like he didn't exist. Then one day, not even a week later, I come into the house with my boys playing again like nothing happened."

"That's horrible and I'm glad it was resolved, but Ms. Emma, what does that have to do with us now?"

"I told you that to say he is an emotional person. He angers quickly but calms down even faster, but when he's hurt, it lasts. And right now, he's hurting and it may last a little while but I

promise you, it will not last for long," Emma said, pleading her case to the woman beside her that looked like she was torn.

"It might not, but how long is not long? Who's to say it won't take months to get over the hurt? Years? I know he loves me, but does he love me enough to work past the hurt and the loss of his wife to be the man that remembers he loves me, too? I'd rather leave now than stay and he grows to resent me."

"I hear you, sweet girl. I just don't want you making rash decisions that can affect you years from now."

"I know and like I said, if it's meant to be, God will make it so," Selena said confidently, even if her face showed worry and uncertainty.

Emma heard her words, but felt in her heart that both of them were making a mistake.

"Baby, he loves you so very much," Emma told her as she embraced her tightly. Selena hugged her back and released a deep breath as she did so.

"And I love him enough to let him go."

"I can't talk you out of this, can I?" Emma asked with a sad but accepting smile to which Selena slowly shook her head no. Emma nodded back and walked the young woman out of the door. The woman she knew was made for eldest son.

When Emma finished talking, Mordecai didn't say a word. He sat still in the rocking chair and stared straight into the front yard.

"She wasn't wrong," he said quietly after minutes of silence. He felt his mother turn towards him, but kept his head and eyes straight before continuing.

"I was so messed up after Ronnie, Mama. I was angry she was dying, sad my kids' mother was leaving me alone to see them grow up, and guilty because I was madly in love with another woman when I shouldn't have even been in the situation to begin with."

"It's what Ronnie wanted, baby. How can you feel guilt from a decision that was mutually made?"

"I don't know, but I did and I don't know what I would have done if she would have tried to talk me out of ending things. It took me years to come out of my funk. You remember. I wouldn't have wanted to resent Selena, but I probably would have because that's how messed up I was."

They settled into silence again before he started to rock in his chair. What he just heard hurt him more than he thought it would and after all these years, the pain hadn't lessened.

"So was that the last time you spoke with her?" he asked after finally turning towards his mother whose intake of breath let him know that he wouldn't like her answer in the slightest. He was proven correct when she shook her head and looked at him with sad eyes.

"A few months later, she called out of the blue. I was so happy because you still hadn't spoken of her to us and you were still mourning and she had moved from her house so I didn't have her number anymore, but that day, she called and I was glad to hear from her," she said with a small, reminiscent smile.

"Oh, baby. I'm so glad to hear from you! How you doin'? You need anything?" Emma called out with a grin that slowly diminished when she heard the sniffles on the other line.

"Hi, Ms. Emma. I'm okay. I was just calling to let you know that I'm still alive and kicking. I know I said I wouldn't totally disappear and didn't want you worrying."

"If you're so okay, then why do I feel like you're close to tears over there?"

Emma heard another sniffle before sobs broke out. Emma's eyes widened before she grabbed the cord of the house phone and wrapped it around her fingers in anxiousness and sat on the stool beside where the phone hung in the kitchen.

"Selena! Talk to me, baby. You're scaring me. What's going on?"

"I'm pregnant, Ms. Emma. I just found out this morning," Selena whispered. Emma gasped and lifted her hand to her mouth in shock.

"I didn't do it purposely and I get that it's horrible timing, but I can't-I can't get rid of my babies," Selena cried. Emma's eyes widened again.

"Babies? Selena, are you having more than one?"

"I'm having two," she whispered. Emma's fingers tugged at the cord harder and wrapped it tighter around her fingers.

"Okay. Okay. What do you want to do?"

They discussed her choices and what needed to happen next. Sadly, Selena wasn't budging on staying away and keeping her children a secret.

"I understand that he's your son, Ms. Emma, but these are my babies. He has two children that need him so much right now, more than I need him, and I know when he looks at our children he'll just see her and our decision to be together. I can't do that to them and I can't do that to me either. I have to be selfish about this and I'm sorry, but I won't change my mind."

It hurt Emma to the core since she knew deep down that Selena was right. Mordecai would support her and would love his children because that's what kind of man he was, but he would be remorseful and maybe even regret making them, even if it was out of love at the time. Because of that, she agreed to stay quiet, but made sure that she was always involved.

From that moment on, she helped Selena financially and emotionally, especially since Selena's own parents had died years before and she was an only child. As the children grew, Emma's guilt did as well, but she never told a soul, not even her husband. As the years passed, she caught word of her son looking to find her again, so she hid Selena and the children and kept her son off of their trail.

That was, until months before, when Selena said she was tired of running and if she was found, she'd deal with the consequences. She was settled in Florida, and was waiting on the knock on the door to let her know she'd been discovered.

Mordecai looked at his mother and didn't know which emotion would show first. He was confused, hurt, angry, and upset. He felt betrayed, but most of all, he felt ashamed. All this time, all of the distance started because he let her get away.

He knew he could be angry with his mother, and he definitely was, but he also knew that this began because he couldn't handle his emotions correctly. He looked at his mother and saw her tear-streaked face and his face softened. She shook her head at him as she spoke.

"I love you son, but as a mother, I couldn't in good conscience go against her. I helped with what I could and I stayed out of her way. They never knew who I was and I never met the children...not until I had to," Emma said with a guilt stricken face.

"Mama, what happened?"

"My baby was in prison and I gave y'all time, but you weren't any closer to getting him out. I needed to get him out," Emma spoke, moreso to herself, but Mordecai was alarmed because he'd never seen his mother so out of sorts.

"Mama, what did you do?" Mordecai asked as he came in front of her and gently grabbed her shaking face in his hands.

"I had to ask, Eloi. I had to ask him to get his brother out of that jailhouse," Emma said as she held on to Mordecai for support.

"What?" Mordecai asked breathlessly before he heard a male's voice come from the front yard. A voice he'd never heard before, but one he immediately knew who it belonged to.

"Damn. I really do look like you, old man."

14

MORDECAI

Mordecai froze and slowly let go of his mother's face before turning around to see the man that the voice belonged to. He stepped off the porch and neared the young man who looked like a younger Chi. He had the same tall, lean build as Mordecai with light skin like his mother with the Jackson signature hazel eyes. Unlike his oldest son, this one had no facial hair which made him look extremely young. Mordecai couldn't stop the tear from falling from his eye as he stopped in front of the young man. His youngest son.

"So? Can I get a hug? Handshake or somethin'?" the young man said with a smirk that made one deep dimple show in his cheek. Mordecai shook his head in amusement before taking one last step and embraced his son in a tight hold.

He felt tears continuously fall from his eyes, but he did nothing to stop them. He heard the screen door close and figured his mother was letting them have their privacy. He squeezed his son one last time before releasing him and wiped under his eyes with the back of his hand.

"I guess you already know who I am," Mordecai said, still feeling emotional after the unexpected meeting.

"Yeah. My mom never told us your name, but we always knew about you. Didn't know too much though. Not 'til Grandma called me and filled in some of the blanks."

"I just-I don't even know where to start."

"Well, first start with not feeling guilty," he answered but Mordecai was already shaking his head in disagreement.

"I'm serious. I can't even lie. When I was a kid, I was mad as hell at you. I was missing my dad. But the older I got, I realized it wasn't your fault, not really. It was a shitty situation all around."

"Yeah, but, you're mine. I've missed out on twenty-two years now. That's everything and I didn't even know," Mordecai said, getting angry all over again.

"I agree. But I'm here now. Find out what you need from me *now* and we'll work on everything else as it comes," he shrugged like it was so simple. Mordecai looked at him and cocked his head towards the house and they walked in together to find Isaiah and Emma whispering in the den.

Isaiah didn't say anything but just stared at his grandson for a few seconds before coming over to them and taking the young man into his arms just as Mordecai had done minutes before. Mordecai glanced at Emma and saw her eyes tear up and saw a small, wobbly smile appear on her face.

"I see my wife has been busy. Everybody take a seat so we can talk," Isaiah instructed before they walked the short distance to the dining room and sat around the table. No one spoke for a while, but the silence was broken when the young man started the much needed conversation.

"We lived in Louisiana for a bit. Probably 'til I was maybe five. My mom worked odd jobs, not because she had since Grandma made sure we were straight, but because she didn't wanna be bored. When we left there, we moved to Mississippi, then Florida. When we moved there, I was maybe ten or eleven, and she started dating this dude. Puerto Rican guy, pretty cool. It got serious and they eventually got married," he told them and Mordecai could feel his blood begin to boil. As if he didn't see his father about to pop a blood vessel, he continued his story.

"He treated my mom like a queen and he cared about us too and things were good. When I was maybe sixteen, he got real sick. It was sudden and there was nothing they could do and he ended up dying a year later. We were devastated, but we had a little time to prepare so we were okay. When it was time to leave for college, I stayed close to my mom to make sure she was good and that's how I first found out about you," he said looking at Mordecai.

"My mom got antsy and paranoid and she started telling me more about you and your family. I can't lie and say I wasn't intrigued. I mean, you sounded like an urban legend or something but she wasn't scared so I wasn't worried. Just anxious, I guess.

"Anyway, years pass and she wants to move again, a different part of Florida this time. I honestly think, looking back, she was ready for you to find her. She loved my step dad, but I don't think she was ever in love with him. But the few times I got her to talk about you? That's how I knew she still wanted you," he shrugged.

Mordecai took in his words and could do nothing but shake his head. He couldn't believe Selena married someone else. He knew he had no right to be upset since it was his fault, but he couldn't help himself. He hoped his son would tell him where she was so he could go get her when all of this was over.

"So how did you and Emma get together?" Isaiah asked.

"Right. I actually reached out to her. I went through my mom's contacts and remembered she always said her name so I found her number and called her. We talked and caught up. It wasn't often that we talked, but I just wanted to be close in a way. Not too long ago, I called and I could tell something was up so when I asked, she finally let me know about Chi being locked up and how much longer he'd be there. I asked what I could do and she told me to make something happen and I did."

"No offense to you, but you're a kid yourself. What exactly could you do?" Isaiah asked, asking the same question Mordecai was curious about as well. Apparently, the question amused him because he gave them a smirk before answering.

"My step dad was the Special Agent in Charge for the Miami Division of the DEA before his death."

"What? What the fuck!" the men hollered at the same time and the young man laughed.

"Yeah. Before him, his father was high up also. So, there was a lot of power there and even though I'm young, he was owed a lot of favors and had a lot of friends in high places. One of those favors and one of those friends got me offered a job before I even graduated college to be in the Chicago Division and I got in the Special Agent in Charge's ear and he let me on the case. I was able to get some of the narcs to speak up about what really happened that day," he said as he sat back in his chair to let the information be soaked in by Mordecai and Isaiah at the table while Emma nervously looked between her husband and son.

"That was incredibly risky," Isaiah finally said.

"But worth it. If I had known my brother was in there, I would have done it a long time ago. I know what y'all do, and I'll be damned if my family is on the wrong side if I can help it."

"So it was you that tipped the paralegal off to go talk to the police again?" Mordecai asked after thinking back months before when he visited his lawyers at their firm.

"Yeah, it was me. You don't have anyone with the DEA here that's high up for some reason, so let's just say, now you do."

He spoke so confidently that Mordecai could do nothing but be proud of him. They were closely intertwined with the government in many capacities, but the DEA wasn't one of their connections. Now, thanks to his son, they were even more secure than before and he was thankful that his son was on their side of things. He glanced over at his mother who already had her eyes on him and she looked pitifully sad. Mordecai couldn't help but laugh.

"Don't give me that look, woman. If you wouldn't have kept all this to yourself, we could have handled it better. I'm mad at you," Mordecai stated and she nodded. "*But*, mad or not, you helped me beyond words and I love you for doing what you thought was best."

His mother bit on her bottom lip to stop from smiling and nodded her head in thanks before Isaiah let them know breakfast was about to be cooked and led Emma into the kitchen. After their exit, the father and son sat and took each other in.

"I have to get your mother," Mordecai announced calmly after a few moments.

"I know," the young man answered.

"Will she...want to come back here?"

"For you? Definitely."

Mordecai nodded with a big sigh of relief. "You know,

you talked about you, but you never said anything about your twin."

"Shit, honestly so much was going through my mind I forgot. My mom named us Malik and Malaya. I was born first and she came about three minutes after."

"Malaya? That's different."

"Yeah, and she hates it. She doesn't ever go by it. Like ever."

"What's she go by then?"

"Her middle name, LaShea."

15

BABY

"Look, I understand why Kiara can't be here, but why do *I* have to be the one in charge of things?" Baby asked his parents who looked around the space that the party would be held in a few days' time.

"Because I said so," Micah said simply as he looked down at his phone, unbothered by his youngest staring him down.

"Mommy. Come on. I'm a man. A very busy man running an almost billion-dollar operation. I don't have time to plan parties. Can't we have a party planner or even tell Moriah to do this?" Baby asked, looking at his mother who walked over to him and began running her hand over his cheek.

"Baby, I love you. You're my youngest and you have half of my heart, so listen when I say this. Suck the shit up and get it done," she said before patting his face twice and stepping back to take her husband's hand.

"Man, fuck this," Baby mumbled but clearly not low enough when Micah's eyes landed on him. He groaned before apologizing to them for his profanity and Renee gave him a sympathetic look.

"It's okay, honey. You do still have Zayne and Zamir helping. And maybe you can get Senai, but you know she's been busy with last minute school business. And we're getting her graduation party together. That's two weeks away, remember?" Renee said sweetly.

"Zayne and Zamir? Mommy, come on now. Zeus won't care as long as it's liquor and women there and Lord's nonchalant ass is just gonna go along with whatever I say just to get done with everything. They're literally useless. Can't we just have a welcome back party at Pop and Grandma's house?" Baby asked, almost whining as Micah smirked at his misery.

"Nope. Chi wants a real get together so this is what we're doing. I said you'd do it because you and Chi are joined at the hip. You talk to him more than D does, almost as much as KiKi. You know him better than a planner and I know you can handle it. I believe in you, Baby, so get it done," Renee said gently but firmly. Just as Baby was about to accept defeat, his dad just had to make it worse.

"Yeah, nigga. Stop bitching," Micah added on with a smirk on his face. Baby wanted to curse him out, but thought better of it. He didn't want to have to fight Micah because he knew his dad wouldn't take it easy on him and he didn't want to have to nurse himself back to health.

"Micah, stop," Renee said sharply and Micah raised his hands in surrender which brought a smirk to Baby's face. Micah may have been the man of the house, but Renee didn't allow him to mess with her children too badly, especially Baby. She always said Messiah could handle it because he was just like his father, but Baby took after her and she wouldn't allow him to bully them if she could help it.

"Your brother will be home in two or three days so he can help you out with anything that you and the other boys don't get done. Senai and Moriah will be around too, but they'll be helping me set the other party up with Senai's family. This is a boys' thing so that's why I wanted the men to take care of it. If it really is too much for you, go get a planner. I don't even care," Renee stated before rolling her eyes at Baby and Micah and walking off.

"Look at what you did," Micah said, watching her walking across the room to talk to the club manager.

"I didn't do a thing, old man. You just like pressing buttons for no reason."

"Whatever. Anyway, you have the budget. Place is paid for and they won't open until the party so you don't have to worry about people coming through here messing up and word's already been spread around so you don't have to worry about advertising. Get the food, get the decorations, and make sure your cousin-in-law doesn't find out. You got this. Chi won't care about much except his family being here anyway so just make it look nice and chill the fuck out," Micah told Baby before he slapped his back and kissed his temple and started his walk across the room to get to Renee.

"Fuck me," Baby groaned lowly as he pulled at one of his long braids in frustration and pulled out his phone so he could call his best friend. He knew his mother told him she was busy, but he needed her help regardless.

"First thing we need to do is get a theme," Senai said as she looked around the club.

"What we need a theme for, Nai? I was just gon' throw some decorations up and call it a day," Baby said with a one-shoulder shrug. Senai looked up at him with exasperation written all over her sienna-toned face.

"Gosh, you're such a man. No, you don't *need* a theme, but why not? It'll make it special and it might keep some of the hoodrats out of here. How about a black tie event or an all-white celebration? You can turn those who don't adhere to the dress code away and it'll look good, too."

"Damn. That actually sounds good. How about Jacksons and other VIPs wear white and everyone else wear black?"

"I like that idea. See? That wasn't all that hard," Senai said with a cocky smile.

"Shut up. I'll get everybody on that though and I'll get them to set up the decorations to match. Wanna go grab some food?"

"Only if you're paying," Senai said, grinning up at him. He sucked his teeth but put his arm over her shoulders and led her out of the club and to his new truck.

"I never would have pegged you as the pickup type," Senai said as she looked around the interior of the truck once he helped her inside.

"Me either, but this is my baby. Plus, I got it fully loaded so it's no different than an SUV."

They talked the entire drive and made it to the restaurant twenty minutes later. He had Senai find a place for them to sit while he went to talk to Ryan who stopped by to update him about one of the traps he ran.

When he walked back into the restaurant, he saw one of his jump offs talking to Senai. He wouldn't have thought much of it, but Senai had a small frown on her face so he rushed over to see what the issue was when he heard the girl "confronting" Senai.

"*...so you need to just leave him alone. I know you wanna*

fuck him or whatever but he don't need you," the girl with a hand on her hip and her neck rolling on her shoulders said.

"Umm, I don't know you so that already tells me you're not as much of a factor as you think you are, but please understand, that one, I'm not going anywhere. And two, just because you suck his dick every other Tuesday night doesn't make you important enough to dish out threats," Senai responded, her light voice tight but not changing in volume.

"Look, hoe. I'm not telling you again. I ain't the one and if I need to handle you, I will," the girl said, getting louder and closer to Senai. Senai didn't get up, but sat up straight in her seat.

"You look like you purposely forgot your home training so I'll excuse your manners, but if you really think you'll handle me, you're even dumber than you look. Now, if you'll excuse me, my friend should be back in a minute and I don't think he'd like you standing so close to me."

"Bitch—"

"Aht aht. You know better," Baby said as he walked to the table and stood in front of the frightened looking girl. Baby had to stop himself from laughing because he could barely remember the girl's last name and she had the audacity to approach somebody.

"The fuck you doin'?" Baby continued staring down at the girl.

"I—I was just talking to her," she stuttered out.

"Talking about what? You don't know her so the fuck you need to talk about?"

"Nothing," she whispered. He could tell she was shaking a little and that pissed him off because she was big and bad when she stepped to Senai.

"Let me find out you a messy one and Ima get my cousin to beat yo ass," Baby threatened and her eyes widened in fear.

Everyone who knew of the Jackson family knew how well they could handle themselves and knew the men didn't touch women, but Moriah would. "Matter of fact, delete my number and if I see you again, I'll handle you myself."

"No, wait. I'm sorry. I ain't mean—"

"Nah. You didn't mean for me to hear you. She ain't the one though so that was your fuck up. I'm not gon' repeat myself," Baby said as he sat in front of Senai. He never looked up at the girl again and finally heard her leave their table.

"You didn't have to do that, you know," Senai addressed him.

"I know I didn't, but that was on me. Why these females get comfortable enough to "woman to woman" other women when they're not even that relevant kills me. Plus, Grandma Althea not about to get on my head 'cause girls coming at you," Baby said with a smirk that had Senai throwing a napkin at him.

"You wouldn't have that issue if you just settled down," Senai told Baby with raised eyebrows.

"Here you go. You know I want to, Nai, but you also know I'm not rushing it either. Hell, I'm only twenty-four. I got time, right?" Baby said after giving his and Senai's orders to the waitress.

"Yes, but that doesn't mean you have to sample the entire female population of Illinois in the meantime. You're better than that," Senai said.

"I know, and you're right. I'm gonna do better," Baby said with a smile that made his left dimple deepen.

"Um hmm," Senai hummed as she sipped on her lemonade.

They continued talking until their food came and they

dug in. Baby knew he shouldn't bring it up, but he felt it was necessary.

"So...Mo told me Scrubs might pop the question. What's up with that?" Baby asked suddenly, making Senai choke on her food. After hitting herself in the chest a few times, she was able to calm down enough to answer him.

"What—Why would you ask that?" she asked wheezingly. Baby rolled his eyes at her dramatics.

"Because it needs to be asked. I know you aren't gonna say yes. Right?"

Senai sighed out as she pushed her plate away from her. "Mecca."

"Don't Mecca me. You know you can't marry that nigga, Nai."

"And why can't I? I've been with him long enough."

"You coulda been with the nigga for twenty years. If you don't love him then you don't need to marry his ass and we all know you don't love him."

"I do love him," she said weakly.

"Yeah? You love him, huh? He make your heart flutter if you haven't seen him in a while? You get excited when you see his name come across your phone? You get this feeling in the pit of your stomach after y'all get into it and just the *thought* of him ending things makes you weak?

"You might love him, but you damn sure not in love with him. That much I do know," Baby said to her. He stared at her and watched as she swallowed hard and put her eyes back on her plate.

"I don't know what to do, Mecca. He's safe and we've been together so long. He makes sense," Senai told him quietly after a few moments of silence.

"I get that. But, what if love isn't always supposed to make sense? Just because you've spent years with this man doesn't mean that you're meant to spend the rest of your life with him. Maybe he was supposed to be a transitional love. Maybe you needed him then and the next man is supposed to be your forever, or maybe not. Either way, settling 'cause you put in time and he's easy doesn't make it right. Nai, you deserve love that doesn't make you crave more and you shouldn't settle for less."

Senai lowered her eyes again and continued to eat her food in silence, but that was okay for Mecca. He knew he gave her a lot to think on. Senai was probably the sweetest person he knew and knew she wouldn't want to hurt anyone's feelings; so much so, that she'd commit to a man she wasn't in love with for the rest of her life just to keep his feelings and ego intact.

Baby didn't want that for her. Even if he thought she and his brother belonged together, if they never happened, he still refused to let her be with a man that he knew didn't deserve her.

If only he could find a woman to love, he'd be all squared away. He'd make sure the people around him were good until then.

16

CHI

Chi took a deep intake of air and could have sworn it had never smelled so fresh. It was finally the day and he couldn't stop smiling. He barely slept the night before, too amped up on the idea of leaving the home he'd had for the past four years. He was up and ready before the guards came to get him from his cell and when he was finally through the gates, he made a promise to himself and to God that he'd never be back again.

He was met by his cousins at his request and almost cried when he hugged Siah and Baby. Even though he spoke with them often and was visited by them frequently, it wasn't nearly the same as being in the free world with them.

"How's it feel, jailbird?" Siah asked after hugging Chi tightly.

"Boy. I don't even have the words," Chi answered, hugging Baby and slapping him on the back a few times.

"We need to hurry up and get you settled 'cause you look like you been in jail for years," Baby said as they hopped in his truck.

"Uhhh, I have or did you forget?" Chi asked with his face balled up.

"Nah, but you actually *look* like you been in there. It's a difference."

"Boy, forget you," Chi told Baby as he and Siah cracked up in the front seat. Chi couldn't keep the smile off of his own face because he missed being able to joke and laugh with his brothers. On top of that, he knew he looked a mess.

They drove back to Chicago, catching up along the way. Chi knew he had a full day ahead of him and had to prepare himself. His welcoming party was that night and he had to make sure his business was good beforehand.

More importantly, he had to get himself right and there was no one better to do that than Renee who would be waiting for him at her house. Chi's clothing for the day and the outfit for the night was already at his uncle and aunt's house so after taking the longest shower imaginable, Chi would get his hair and beard trimmed up and get dressed afterwards.

"My baby," Renee sobbed as soon as Chi stepped through the door. She held him tightly and he could feel nothing but love coming from her. He had missed her presence so much he found himself getting emotional. Micah didn't allow Renee to visit too often and he agreed. It did keep him from seeing her as often as he liked, but a reunion like this made it worth it.

Micah came over to calm her down and once she was back together, she hugged him one more time and smiled up at him and told him to go relax. She didn't have to tell him twice before he hugged his uncle and took off to Siah's room. He saw the bed and wanted to dive in, but knew he had to wash the prison smell and feeling off of him so he headed to the bathroom.

Even with having more privileges than the other inmates, Chi still said a quick prayer of thanks when he stepped into the shower. He stood with his head facing the ceiling and his eyes closed as he let the water from the rainfall shower head douse him from head to toe.

After standing under the water for forty minutes, he had the water come from the hand held shower head and washed his body over and over until he felt completely clean before getting out. He felt renewed as he stepped out and patted his body down and moisturized himself before brushing his teeth.

He told himself that he was ready for his haircut so he could get his day started, but when he was back in the bedroom, he couldn't stop himself from going over to the bed and staring down at it in contemplation.

"Rest," Micah said gently as he came to stand in the doorway. "Party's not until nine tonight and it's a little after ten. You've got time."

"Yeah, but I got a lot to do and—"

"Malachi," Micah said with firmness. Chi could do nothing but look over to his uncle who had a stern look on his face but eyes filled with love and concern. "Sleep. We got everything until you're good."

With that, Micah left him and he could do nothing but shake his head with a small smile on his face. Micah was tough with them, but he also was the one that babied them when he felt it necessary. His father showed them love as well, but didn't think babying and "coddling" them as he put it was the way to go.

He couldn't wait to see him later either, but knew Mordecai was busy getting his new home together. Kiara didn't know it, but they'd be moving soon. His father was also getting him a new vehicle and anything else he thought

Chi needed. He smirked at that. He might not baby the boys, but he definitely had a way about him.

He tugged the covers back and literally fell into the bed with a moan. Siah always had the best mattress and even though he rarely stayed there when he was in Chicago, he made sure he had one in the house that was ridiculously comfortable. Not even five minutes later, he was out like a light.

"Damn, boy. You wanna sleep the day away?" Chi heard someone ask. It took a few moments to get out of his sleepy spell, but when the voice registered, a smile slid across his face. He peeled his eyes open to see his dad looking down at him.

"D, leave him alone. He's allowed to sleep," Renee fussed as she stepped into the room. She was only five-foot-nine but stood in front of Mordecai with her hands on her wide hips like she matched his impressive height of six-six.

"Sis, y'all let the boy sleep the whole afternoon."

"Just because you don't like to sleep, doesn't mean he doesn't. Now, get out," she said as she shooed him away. Mordecai looked back at him with narrowed eyes and left the room.

"Thanks, Mama. You know his grumpy ass wasn't gon' leave me alone otherwise," Chi said with a laugh as he sat up and rubbed his eyes.

"I already know. But he just missed you and wanted to bother you," Renee answered as she came over to inspect his hair and beard. He closed his eyes as she massaged his scalp. She always had a way to calm his spirit and he missed it like crazy while he was away.

"I think the long beard look works for you. Makes you look mature," she said sweetly. He couldn't help but smile because his aunt really was one of the sweetest people he knew. The only one who halfway measured up would be Senai, which was probably a lot of the reason his cousin was so in love with her.

He grabbed her hand which was still massaging his head and kissed her wrist which made her tear up. He used to do it as a kid because he didn't say he loved people that often, but it was his way of saying so.

"I missed you, Mama."

"I missed you, too. But, it's okay because you're not leaving again."

"I'm definitely not leaving again."

"Good. Now, get dressed before your daddy brings his ass back in here. Siah put some Nike tracksuits you can wear in his closet 'til you get to shop on your own. You're bigger now so you might even be able to fill one out," she said jokingly as she started to walk out of the room.

"His big ass still has me by at least twenty-five pounds so I don't know," Chi laughed and so did Renee.

When he was dressed, he made his way to the living room to find Mordecai, Micah, and Renee talking and Siah and Baby watching television. He took a second to take it all in before announcing himself.

"Yo yo yo!"

"Calm all that shit down!" Mordecai yelled out with his face balled up. Siah and Baby cracked up from the couch while Chi rolled his eyes at his father's antics. He knew Mordecai missed him and was playing it off with being cranky. It was okay, though. Chi would get on his nerves daily and the idea of how many things he could do brought a smirk to his face.

He noticed a plate of food on the table that his father tilted his head toward and took a seat. He hadn't had a home cooked meal in years and had to stop himself from getting emotional as he inhaled the breakfast on his plate. When he finished his food, he downed his orange juice before getting up and leaning down to kiss the top of Mordecai's head and hugged his shoulders.

"Come on, Chi. Let me get you set so you can handle your business," Renee called over to him as she stood from the table so she could get her clippers and scissors ready.

He took a seat and let her drape the cape over his body. He'd luckily washed his head and beard in the shower so it was one less step his aunt had to go through. She massaged the mass of kinks on top of his before she began to cut it down. Chi would miss his little fro but missed his waves more.

He got occasional clips while he was knocked, but never let anyone get close to his scalp because he didn't trust anyone but his aunt. Twenty minutes later, he saw his waves were back and couldn't contain the dimpled grin on his face.

"How low do you want this?" Renee questioned as she pulled on his beard. He wanted it as short as Siah's, whose beard was full but not too far off of his face, but Kiara said she liked it longer so he'd have to accept having a longer beard until she got tired of it.

"You can cut it about two inches, Mama. Ari wants it off my chin a little bit so I still need some length," he told her with a grimace to which she laughed and got her scissors and beard clippers together.

Another fifteen minutes and Chi was out of the chair feeling like a new man. He tried to give Renee money for his cut and she looked at him like he was crazy so he laughed and kissed her cheek. He knew she didn't take money from family, but he thought he'd try anyway.

"Alright, I'm out. I'll be back a little later to get dressed,"

Chi called out and Baby got up to follow him out of the door.

Chi knew he had to get a new license, but he'd worry about it the following Monday. Until then, he'd let Baby drive him around. They discussed the streets and how they were looking until they made it to the warehouse. Baby had only informed their lieutenants about Chi's early release, so all their soldiers would be in for a surprise.

"Damn, it's good to see your pretty boy ass out in the world," Benny called out as they got out of Baby's truck before they gave each other a hug.

"Now, we both know the only pretty one is this nigga," Chi said nodding his head in Baby's direction. They laughed while Baby shot him the bird.

"Cousin! Man, it's been too long," Ryan called out as he approached the group. He was technically only related to Siah and Baby because Renee and his father were siblings, but he claimed all of the Jacksons as family and the same went for Chi.

They embraced before Chi asked where the other three lieutenants were so they could get the meeting over with. They informed him they were already waiting so they all walked inside.

"Nah, don't get quiet on my account," Chi called out when he walked in front of his workers and his presence had them completely silent. As he looked around, he saw some have reverence on their faces while others seemed more afraid than anything else.

"For those that don't know me because you came to the family after my...absence, my name is Chi. I've always been around and that's not changing. I've heard good things about you all so let's keep it that way and we won't have any problems," Chi spoke before he heard a muffled voice speak.

It was quiet in the warehouse so he heard it pretty easily, but wasn't sure what was said.

"Somebody got something to say?" Chi asked the group, trying to find the voice, but no one spoke up. He glanced at Baby and saw him looking at the group as well, but didn't seem to catch anything either.

"Good. Didn't need any problems before we got back friendly," Chi threw out to them before sending a haunting smile their way. Just as he was about to turn around, he heard the muffled voice again, but this time, saw the young man who said something before he could hide.

"You got shit to say, bruh?" Chi asked as he slowly walked over to the guy. The man he was hiding behind widened his eyes before he looked up at Chi who told him to move over with a nod of his head to the side. The man hurriedly slid over leaving Chi face to face with a young man he'd never seen before, but couldn't have been any older than twenty or twenty-one.

"Ion know you to have a problem, so you can move out my face," the young man said as he looked up at Chi. He couldn't have been over five-foot-eight but stood strong and Chi could do nothing but respect it. What he couldn't do was accept the disrespect the young man was throwing his way.

"Whose soldier is this?" Chi asked without taking his eyes off of him.

"He's mine," one of Benny's men gritted out. Chi turned to see him and saw he was staring a hole through the young one's head.

"You can let him know who I am or you can make sure he doesn't step foot on my streets again. I don't care which," Chi addressed him before turning back to the young buck who was clenching his jaw in front of him.

"You got heart. I like that, but what you need to learn is when to bow out. I'm the Head Nigga In Charge over here and the fact you got slick for no reason shows me you might not be for this long term. It's cool though 'cause a lot of you don't know me, but if you do that shit again, I'll kill you myself."

Without waiting for a response, he turned to walk back to the front where Baby was waiting with a subtle smirk on his face. He'd only been out a few hours and was already annoyed, but he was also happy to be back home to deal with things up close and personal. It was time to get his kingdom back.

17

KIARA

"Mommy," Mercy whined.

"What's wrong, Ci-Ci?" Kiara asked as she came to stand in her daughter's doorway. She looked down and saw Mercy playing with her big LEGOs. Kiara made sure her baby had actual toys and not just electronic devices to keep her busy. She was glad Mercy preferred real toys.

"I want Daddy. Can I call?"

"I wish we could, but Daddy is a little busy today, remember? He promised he'd talk to us tomorrow," Kiara told her gently, but still got a pitiful pout in return. Kiara hated it, but knew it wasn't much she could do.

Chi texted her the night before saying they had to go on lockdown again because of a fight that had broken out and wouldn't be able to talk to them until the next day. She knew how things could be unpredictable on the inside so she sulked inwardly. Mercy on the other hand, was too young to understand and made her grievances known.

"Otay," she answered back sadly. Kiara almost laughed at

how put out her daughter looked and sounded but thought better of it; it would only make matters worse.

"You get to see Auntie Eshe today. Are you excited?" Kiara asked after watching her for a few moments. Mercy looked up with her hazel eyes widened and nodded enthusiastically, her sadness temporarily forgotten, making Kiara laugh.

Eshe was Kam's older sister who lived in Brooklyn. There was a party that the girls wanted her to go to that "she just couldn't miss" and needed a babysitter. Her mother was out of town with her uncle Reggie and Mordecai, Micah, and Renee were also busy. Isaiah and Emma had been out of town for a few days, also. Luckily, her aunt was coming to visit them and said she'd gladly keep her great niece for the night.

"Good. Now go wash up and come eat your breakfast," Kiara said and watched her baby run to her bathroom to wash her hands and run back to her.

"Don't you think this is a little short?" Kiara asked her girls who were all looking approvingly.

"Hell, not short enough," Andrea said as she sipped her mimosa. Kiara gave her a long look which she ignored. If she bent over, all of her cheeks would be hanging out, but it wasn't short enough?

"Whose thing is this anyway? And why do we all have to wear white? I have a bomb ass orange dress that gives my skin a pregnancy glow without being pregnant hanging up in my closet," Kiara said as she looked at the dress again in the mirror.

"You are asking a hell of a lot of questions, Ki. Just know

this party is about to be the shit and we gotta turn heads. You know how we do," Moriah answered as she put the dress she was holding up to her body.

Kiara rolled her eyes while she threw the dress off of her and eyed another dress that was on her bed. She liked the cut of the dress and decided to try it on. While she rolled the dress over her hips, she heard her alarm go off and figured it was Senai coming in.

"Sorry I'm late—Oh! Wow, Ki. That dress is everything," Senai said as she looked at Kiara. Kiara looked in the mirror and liked what she saw. Andrea and Moriah also gave their praises.

"I think this is the one," Kiara said as she turned to look at them. The v-cut off the shoulder bodycon dress looked painted on, but was still classily sexy. It did nothing to hide her assets and was high on her thighs, but she knew it was the right decision.

They nodded in agreement and she took the dress off and put back on her sweats. They still had hours to go before they needed to get ready and were going to chill until then.

"WHAT THE HELL! Why so many people here?" Kiara asked as she looked out of the window and saw the long line of people trying to get into the club.

"It's the place to be, boo. Everybody wanna be in tonight," Andrea said as she parked her car.

They got out and made their way to the front of the club. Kiara thought it odd that the parking lot was full but Andrea was able to get a park with ease, but shook the thought away. She was going to enjoy her night and look fine while doing so and was happy she wouldn't have too far to go in her too high heels.

Once they were in, she looked around the lower level of the club and couldn't help the furrow of her eyebrows. She saw everyone wearing black and looked back at Senai with a questioning glance and received a soft smile in return. Before she could ask about the dress code, she was pulled towards the stairs by Andrea.

When they reached the top floor, she saw other people besides her and her girls wearing white and felt a little better. That was until she saw who it was wearing it.

"I thought you said you were busy tonight so you couldn't watch your grandbaby?" Kiara asked Mordecai, who stood beside Micah, both wearing suits without ties and Micah without a suit jacket with his sleeves rolled up at the elbows.

"This was me being busy, Kiara. Pretty good excuse, I think," he said calmly, lifting his glass to drink but keeping his playful hazel eyes on her.

She narrowed her eyes at him and his brother who gave her a smile and a wink before she turned to look for the group she came with but didn't see them anywhere. She let her father-in-law and uncle-in-law know they were on her shit list; all they did was laugh and she narrowed her eyes even more. She looked around and spotted Siah, Baby, and the Andrews brothers in the corner and went to speak with them until her girls reappeared.

"Why are you the only one up here wearing black?" Kiara asked Zeus as she walked up to the group.

"You know I don't do white, KiKi. I'm a dark nigga that likes dark things," Zeus answered with a shrug. Kiara rolled her eyes before looking over at Siah and Baby. They both looked nice, Baby more casual with jeans and a button down. Siah, as usual, looked like money in a satin dress shirt and dress pants.

"Whose party is this? I know you know," she asked, looking up at Baby. He smirked before answering her.

"Why I gotta be the one to know?"

"Because you always know."

"Ha! Yeah, that is true."

"....well? Whose is it?"

Before he could answer, she was pulled away to dance. Her girls claimed they had gone to the bathroom while she was talking to Mordecai and Micah and had just gotten back situated. She thought it was weird it took so long, but didn't speak on it. It was a lot of people in attendance after all.

An hour later, she was winding her hips and singing along to the mix the deejay had going. She had been sipping cocktails and was feeling good. She lifted her arms in the air and was moving seductively when she felt someone come behind her and grab her waist. She tried to turn to tell them off, but her waist was gripped tighter.

"I've been over there watching you for the past hour and I must say that ass is sitting right. Thighs looking a lil small, but I'll take care of that soon," she heard a voice whisper in her ear. Her breath caught in her throat and her lips quivered. She was finally allowed to turn around and heard a whimper leave her lips.

She had so many things to say, but she couldn't find the words. He must have realized she was stuck because he smiled the smile that made her fall for him.

"Hey, Ari. You missed me?"

After staring at him for a full minute, her mind finally snapped from the haze it was in and she didn't know which emotion she wanted to unload first. When he sent a dimpled smirk her way, she chose anger.

"What the fuck are you doing here?" she asked with a punch to his chest. When he didn't immediately answer, she started hitting him over and over, continuing her questions of how and why he was there. When all of her anger and shock were gone, her feelings melted into being so happy that tears spilled from her eyes with Chi wiping them away as they fell with a soft smile on his face.

"Mal, how?" she asked again after she calmed down. He had already moved them to an empty corner of the VIP section so they could have the privacy to talk.

"I got out early," he said simply with a shrug. He must have seen she was about to ask more questions because he continued. "We already figured I was set up, but what we didn't know was that the cops were in on it and they came in with an unsigned warrant. It took awhile to figure it out, but once Scottie and his team did, they worked on getting me out sooner."

"Wow. How long have you known?"

"A few months."

Kiara was hurt. So hurt, she tried to get up, but Chi wouldn't let her.

"I didn't want to tell you for two reasons. One being that I didn't want to get your hopes up just for something to go wrong. And two, I wanted to surprise you. Aren't you surprised?"

"Well, yes. I guess so. But I still wanted to know. So this is your party?" she asked, looking around. Now that she actually noticed the people on the upper level, it was filled with only family, friends, and higher ups that worked within the Jackson organization.

"Yep, all mine, bae. Baby set it up even though I think Sen and Siah did all the work."

"How the hell did I not know about this? It's a big ass

deal and from the line that I saw coming in here, everybody in Chicago knew about it," she asked, looking at him in scrutiny.

"That was actually pretty easy. We made sure nobody around you would say anything. Plus, you don't do social media so it was easy to hide it," Chi answered amusingly. Kiara sucked her teeth. She had an Instagram but rarely checked it so of course she would have missed any news.

"I just can't believe it," Kiara said as she gazed over at him making sure he was actually there. And there he was, dressed in an outfit similar to Siah's, except Chi also had a coat to match.

"Believe it, Ari. And we can talk about all the ins and outs all night long while I'm in and out of you," he responded smoothly with another smirk.

"Ha. Clever," she said dryly. He laughed hard and tugged her over to him and sat her on his lap.

"In the morning when we go get my baby, we're getting out of Illinois for a few days," he said after a few moments of her playing with his beard.

"In the morning?"

"I was dead ass serious about being in you all night. My first night as a free man and I refuse to do anything else. Besides, Eshe already knows what's up."

"She's in on this, too?"

"Duh. Pops, Uncle Micah, Mama Renee, Grandma, Pop, your mom, and your uncle daddy are all here somewhere, or was at some point or another."

"He is not my uncle daddy, boy."

"I mean...he kinda is, Ari. He's your uncle and he's technically been your stepdaddy for some years," he answered with a shrug. She gave him a dirty look and he pecked her lips.

"I'm glad you're home. Promise you won't go away again."

"Only God himself can take me away from you. Even then, I'd try my hardest to stay."

"Good enough for me," she told him before hopping up and dragging him back over to the others.

She never would have thought her night would end like this, but she did say she was going to enjoy it.

18

MORIAH

"TeeTee, did you hear me?"

"Yeah C-Baby, I got you. You and Mommy and Daddy should be back home soon so we can do something then, okay?" Moriah compromised with her niece.

Chi had taken Kiara and Mercy to Orlando to go to Disney World and Mercy didn't want to leave. She was so stuck on staying that Mercy called her to try and get her to join them. She was able to talk her down, but only with a promise that they'd have girl time when she came back home.

"Otay, Daddy said we gotta eat now, so bye. Love you!"

"Love you, too, Mercy," Moriah answered but Mercy had already hung up the FaceTime. She shook her head and got her purse and work ID to go into her building.

She was still reeling from her brother coming home days before, but it was time to get back to her reality. She made it to her office after speaking to some of her coworkers and saw she had a few new folders in the file holder outside of her office door. She exhaled a quick sigh before setting her purse in her desk drawer and sliding her heels off of her feet. She could tell her day would be long.

Even though she was a mental health counselor for a private facility, her workload was still hectic. She normally had to work with children that were referred by private schools and academies or children that came on the radar of attorneys through cases they were on. She hadn't received a child that was in dire need of help, but knew she had to stay on top of her game just in case.

"Hi, yes. My name is Moriah Jackson. I visited with you last Monday? I was calling to check in on Chasity Meyers," Moriah spoke into the phone with the foster parent she'd met with a week before.

"Thank you for returning my call. You know Chasity doesn't really speak much and I was wondering if there was anything in her file that she had at her old home that made her feel better? I want her as comfortable as possible," came the voice of the new foster dad. Moriah couldn't help but smile at his hesitant words. Moriah advocated for black couples to adopt and foster and knew the older couple she'd met would be perfect.

"Yes, actually. She had a little stuffed Barney dinosaur she always had, but it got lost when they took her from her home. Maybe getting another would help her adjust?"

"That's perfect. Thank you so much," he said to her. They spoke for a few more minutes before she ended the call and checked the other files she had. While typing information into her computer, she had a knock on her door.

"Hey, you," she said to Derrick who looked like a piece of chocolate she wanted to devour.

"Hey, honey. I know you said you were going to be busy today so I just wanted to stop by for a second," Derrick said as he came farther into her office.

"Aww, Der. I'm never too busy for you. How's your morning so far?" she asked as she rounded her desk to give him a kiss.

"Productive. I've been training Haven all morning so a break was needed."

"Ahh, yes. Another amazing day of fun with Ms. Kakoa," Moriah said sarcastically.

"Don't do that. You have no reason to act like that," Derrick told her, trying, and failing, to reprimand her.

"You mean besides her desire to hump you 'til she can't anymore? Yeah, guess you're right," she said as she walked back to sit at her desk.

"Moriah, please. I only want you and only want you humping me. You know that," he said quietly.

"Yes, I know that, Derrick. Doesn't mean I'm not blind to what's around me, though. I'll be good for now. Promise."

"Good girl. I'll see you later?"

"Yep. I'll be by around seven," she told him before he reached across her desk to peck her lips again and left her office. She blew out a breath through her nose and closed her eyes for a moment.

"Why does it always feel like the person that hasn't done anything has to be the one being the bigger person?" she murmured to herself.

~

"And then I have to hear about this damn girl from some of the other men in the office. She just does too much, Nai," Moriah pouted to her best friend while they looked around the store.

She left work earlier than she planned because she was annoyed at hearing Haven's name wherever she went. She'd come to work yet again in a highly inappropriate ensemble of a too-short dress and hooker heels and even if her man didn't acknowledge her, she knew Derrick looked. How could he not?

"Moriah, stop this. You're literally an Amazonian goddess in the flesh. You're beautiful and sexy and smart and honestly one of the best people I know. If he wanted her over you, you shouldn't even want him. Clearly, it would be something missing with the man upstairs," Senai said as she tapped her temple with her pointer finger.

"I hear what you sayin' sis, but it's just something about her. It's not paranoia and it's not insecurity. It's just this gut feeling, ya know?"

"I get it." Before Moriah could dive deeper into the issues of her relationship, she saw the cutest handbag that would be perfect for Senai.

"Ahhh! Nai, look," Moriah said as she looked at her friend who was already shaking her head.

"Moriah, no. I came here to look and help *you* find something to wear for the party. You know I'm not spending three thousand dollars on a bag," Senai said even as she looked at the Saint Laurent bag with longing.

Unlike Moriah, Senai was very practical with her money, especially when it came to fashion. She had nice things, of course, but she didn't spend thousands at a time unless she had to. Usually, she'd get talked into buying something nice for herself, like now, if Moriah could get her with the right words.

"Think of it as an early graduation gift to yourself. And you haven't gotten anything in awhile so it's not like you're over spending. And if it helps, I'll get a bag, too," Moriah told her as she picked up a handbag she'd been eying since they came into the store. She looked over at Senai who was fidgety and biting her lip before slowly nodding.

"I knew it wouldn't take much to change your mind. Now, we can check out. I have my shoes already so I'm good to go," she grinned at her friend as she grabbed her hand and led her to the counter.

"Can you please make sure Daddy D has the entire menu covered? If not, I can get him some more help," Senai said as Moriah dropped her back off at their apartment. Even though Senai could have any kind of food for her graduation party, all she wanted was barbecue so of course Mordecai, Micah, and Jonathan were going all out for her.

"Girl, please. Daddy and our uncles got this. Plus, our grandmas, Mama, and Auntie Kam are doing the sides and desserts. If anything, we'll probably have enough leftovers to last us for the Fourth."

"I just wanna make sure everything is taken care of. Anyway, I'll see you tonight?" Senai asked as she jumped out of the Jeep and Moriah nodded her answer. She waved her goodbye before she took off to Mordecai's.

"Daddy!" she yelled when she stepped through the back door. She shouted for him again and heard him coming towards the kitchen.

"Why every time you come home, you gotta be loud?" Mordecai asked her as he stepped towards her and gave her a kiss on the forehead.

"I just wanted to make sure you were alive in here. What are you doing anyway?" she asked as she followed him towards his bedroom. She saw he had clothes out as if he was going somewhere.

"Gotta go handle some business out of town so I'm leaving in a few," he told her as he went back to getting his things together.

"But the party—"

"Isn't 'til Saturday night. It's only Monday. I'll be back by then."

"Promise?"

"Promise."

She looked at her dad and she felt like something was off with him. He'd been quiet lately, more withdrawn. She didn't know if something was bothering him or if she was just reading too much into nothing.

"You're okay, right? Nothing's wrong?" she asked hesitantly. He stopped packing and looked over at her and gave her a smile that let her know that he wasn't dying but something was still going on. She knew him too well to think otherwise.

"I'm fine, Peanut. If all things go as planned, I'll make sure to tell you when I get back."

"And if they don't go as planned?"

"I'm still telling you. Just won't be as happy about it," he answered. She was about to ask more questions, but knew from the look he gave her that she wouldn't get any answers. They talked until he was finished getting his things packed and he walked her out and to her car, with his bag in his hand.

"I love you. Please be careful and be safe."

"I love you, too and no worries. Your old man can handle whatever comes his way," he said before hugging her tightly and giving her another kiss.

She backed out of the driveway slowly and looked at her father again as he got into his own vehicle and said a silent prayer for him. Something was up. She only hoped it wasn't bad news.

19

MORDECAI

ordecai pulled his rental in front of the driveway of the quaint home. He'd landed in Jacksonville an hour earlier and took his time getting a rental vehicle and getting to his location. He hadn't felt nervousness in years. Then again, anything dealing with Selena Richardson brought out feelings and emotions he didn't feel often.

When he landed, he called his brother to talk and confess what he was up to. Not surprisingly, Micah already had a feeling he had a woman all those years ago. He was shocked to learn about his children, but was ready to meet them whenever Mordecai was ready to introduce them.

He knew he had procrastinated long enough so he took a deep breath and got out of the SUV, walked the path to the front door, and knocked. Not two minutes later was he holding his breath as he looked into the eyes of the woman that stole his heart all those years ago.

"It took you long enough," Selena said after a minute of looking him over. She slid the door open wider so he could walk through and gently closed it behind him. She led them into her living room while he looked around and felt auto-matically at peace. She'd always had a way about her that made wherever she was feel like home.

When she got to the couch, she took a seat and took a tentative glance towards him. He was still looking at her with his bottom lip tucked between his teeth, making his deep dimples come to the surface. He finally took a seat next to her and reached over for her hand. Surprisingly, she let him take it.

"I've been looking for you," he told her, keeping his voice as light and soft as possible, as he looked hard at her hand. Still soft as ever, he noticed she wasn't wearing the wedding ring that her late husband gave her. He looked up at her and saw her blush and nod her head slowly.

"I know."

"Why didn't you tell me, Lena?"

"I don't know. When they were babies, I felt it was too soon. When they were teenagers, I figured too much time had passed. I didn't want them hurt and I didn't know how you'd feel," Selena said as her voice cracked with emotion.

"Baby, you should have told me. Told me something—anything. I've missed so much of their lives, hell, your life," he told her. He was still angry and still hurt behind her actions as well as his own. He squeezed her hand when he felt her try to tug it away from him.

"I'm sorry. I've lived with the guilt for so long. Shea was under me so much she wasn't overly questioning when it came to not knowing her dad, but Malik—he wanted to know you so badly. He acts just like you. Same temper, same sense of humor, same mentality. I kept them away from you, and I understand if you can't forgive me for that," she said, whispering the last part. He realized she was crying and pulled her into his lap.

"I won't lie and say I ain't mad 'cause I am. But, I do get it so I'll get over it. What I won't get over so easily though, is you marrying somebody else," he jokingly said. She rolled her eyes and shook her head as she sniffled. She looked him in his eyes and he felt like a piece of himself had reappeared after being gone for so long.

"It took you too long to get me so yes, I got married. And I loved him, too," Selena told him which made him ball his face up, but she grabbed his chin to make him look at her. "But you never left my heart. He knew that and was okay with it. He was my best friend and biggest supporter, and for that, I could never thank him enough."

"Um hmm. I guess he was aight then," he said as he pushed her hair behind her ear and kissed her temple. He looked at her for a while, taking in her beauty and how well she'd aged over the years. "You know you coming back with me, right?"

"Wait, what?"

"What? You thought I was coming just to visit you? Come on now."

"Eloi—"

"Nope. Don't wanna hear that shit. Pack whatever you wanna take with you and leave everything else."

"I can't just leave my house. It's mine!"

"Ohhh, so you raised your voice with yo new man? Ima have to work that outta you, huh?" he asked her with a smirk. She didn't respond, but he noticed she couldn't stop the blush that flushed her cheeks. He was happy to know his words still affected her.

"And I never said you had to sell your home, baby. You comin' home with me, but your house is yours to do what you want with it. I promise."

"Um. Fine. What am I supposed to tell my kids?"

"*Our* kids will be aight. Malik already knows and I have to meet LaShea. I'm guessing you knew she was close to my nephew?" After thinking about the name after Malik told him and seeing a photo Malik had of her, he realized who she was and how he'd had so many opportunities to meet his daughter, but the timing never worked out.

"Yeah. I almost died when she told me the first time, but maybe it was God's will that led her to her family."

"Maybe so, baby. Maybe so."

"I KNEW yo sneaky ass was hiding something," Micah said with a smirk.

"Fuck you, I ain't hide shit. I just didn't tell you," Mordecai said as he playfully shoved his brother.

"But for real, she's a good look, D. Meek little thing but a good look nonetheless."

"Yeah, that's my baby. I gotta make up for lost time somehow."

"Take her to our spot for a minute," Micah said as he looked over at Renee talking Selena's head off. Mordecai looked at his brother in question after thinking about what he said.

"Me and Renee can handle things here for a while. Hell, Chi is back home and jumped right back in so business is taken care of. You need to get yo woman right and if taking her out the country for a minute does that, then you need to do it."

"Yeah. I'll think about it. I need to meet my daughter first and then introduce all my kids to each other before I decide anything," he said and grimaced afterwards. He could only imagine how the meeting would go.

"Would not wanna be you when that happens," Micah told him as they both walked over to their women. Micah walked behind Renee and pulled her to him while Mordecai walked beside Selena and held her by her waist.

"Baby, I was just telling Selena how she could paint some art for the shop and some of the businesses we have since she won't have anything to do for awhile. What you think?" Renee asked Micah. Everyone knew Micah would go along with whatever she said, but she always liked asking his input anyway.

"Yeah, that sounds good, mama. You paint, Selena?"

"I do, yes. I do a lot of Black art nowadays. I figured since he kidnapped me I might as well make myself useful and maybe sell some pieces," she said as she shyly glanced up at him with a small smile on her face.

"Oh, for sure. You family so we support each other. Just let us know what you need and we got you. Me and Reeny getting outta here. I need to holla at my youngest and she gotta finish setting up for this party," Micah said before dapping up with Mordecai and giving Selena a hug and a kiss to her cheek. Renee did the same and they left the house.

"That went better than I thought it would," Selena said as she relaxed in his bed. They'd only gotten back into town that morning after familiarizing themselves with each other again the day before. As soon as they got settled, he called his parents, kids, and his brother and let them know he was back and Micah came right over to meet his sister-in-law, at least she would be if Mordecai had any say about it.

"I told you he'd love you."

"Yeah. And his wife is just amazing. She's so friendly and it seemed genuine," Selena said with a smile on her face.

"That's Renee for you. You'd think being with a boss all

these years would have toughened her up, but nope. Still a sweetheart that could literally make friends with anybody," he said as he glided over towards his side of the bed and got in beside her.

"Think you can be happy here? With me?" he asked after playing with her hair for a few moments. She turned to look at him and all he saw was the love and adoration in her eyes that he used to see before he sent her away.

"I'd be happy with you wherever."

"Good. Because you need to get used to being in Chicago again. And afterwards, we need to see if we can set up a meeting for our kids. Let's just hope it doesn't blow up in my face."

"I wasn't here before, but I'll be here every step of the way this time. I promise."

"That's what I like to hear. But come over here and show me you mean it," he said as he lifted her up and made her straddle him as she giggled softly into their kiss.

20

SENAI

"Damn, girl. If I wasn't strictly dickly, I would literally be drooling over you right now," Moriah said as she finished Senai's makeup.

"Can you control yourself for just a moment, please?" Senai said with a shake of her head, but couldn't stop the blush from spreading on her skin.

"How can I? Babes. You really do look amazing," Moriah said a little softer. Moriah pulled her from her seat so she could stand in front of the full body mirror and she had to do a double take.

She wore a brown satin cowl neck dress that hugged her small breasts and seemed painted on over her curves. The brown satin was a perfect complement against her sienna skin and with the natural beat Moriah did on her face, even she could see she looked like a doll.

Instead of having her hair blown out or in a ponytail like she normally wore it, she decided to wear it in its natural state, so her kinky afro was huge and hung well past her shoulders with a small part down the middle of it.

She would also be wearing some gold strappy stiletto heels that tied around her ankles when it was time for them to leave. They were a graduation gift from Moriah that almost made her cry because she had been eying them for a while, but would never pay so much for one pair of shoes. Her best friend however surprised her with them before they started getting ready for her party and she couldn't express her gratitude enough.

"Now, it's almost eight. Is there anything else you need to take care of before we get ready to go?" Moriah asked her as she finished putting her hair in a slick bun on the top of her head.

"No, no. I think that's it. I'm a little nervous," Senai confessed.

"You shouldn't be. This is just family and friends. People you've been around damn near your whole life celebrating this amazing achievement that you've worked hard for. You deserve this time to shine," Moriah said as she came to give Senai a hug. "Now let's take a pic for the Gram. I'm much too fine to not be seen by the world."

Senai laughed and posed with her friend as she took picture after picture. They were sipping on some wine when they got a knock on their door and knew it was time for them to go.

The men didn't want them to drive so one of the soldiers would be their driver for the night. Senai thought it was unnecessary but knew better than to protest. They'd just ignore her anyway.

She looked down at her phone and saw she had a text from Warren saying he would be a little late but would definitely be there. She smiled softly at the next message he sent because it was a sweet poem he'd read that made him think of her. She hadn't seen him in a week so she was glad he'd be there.

"Aight. Boss man said he was meeting you at the door so just go on in and he should be standing there," the soldier said as he helped them out of the car. They nodded their thanks and headed inside the club.

"Took y'all long enough," Chi scolded as they made their way over and hugged him. Kiara was tucked under him and gave each of them a huge hug and made sure they knew she loved their outfits. Kiara left Chi standing in the foyer area and walked the girls inside. Senai was laughing at something Kiara was telling them when she stopped in her tracks at the scene in front of her.

Everyone yelled congratulations at the top of their lungs and confetti was released into the air. Senai had to fan her face to keep the tears at bay. There were decorations, balloons, congrats signs, and huge pictures of her at her white coat, undergrad, and high school graduations. She'd helped plan her party, but had no idea that the end result would leave her so emotional.

There was also a blown up photo of her parents that caused the lump in her throat to grow even more. She'd had her ceremony the previous Thursday, but to actually celebrate with her loved ones made it all the more surreal.

After making her rounds, Senai went to her grandmother Althea's table, where she and Emma were sitting.

"I'm so proud of you, baby. First doctor in the family," Emma told her with a proud smile.

"Thank you, Grandma Emma," Senai responded with a full blown grin. Emma was like another grandmother to her and Senai loved that she had so much support.

"Senai?"

"Yes, Grammy?"

"Warren is here. He'll probably be coming for you in a little bit."

"Oh, good. I haven't seen him yet."

"No, suga. He's *coming* for you, if you catch my drift," Althea said with a raise of her eyebrows that made Senai's eyes widen and heart speed up. She nodded her head and walked briskly towards her girls after telling them she'd be back a little later.

"What's wrong with you?" Kiara asked as soon as she noticed Senai's facial expression.

"It's happening," Senai whisper-yelled over the music.

"Uhh, wanna be more specific?" Moriah asked with a confused look.

"I think—"

"Baby! There you are. I was looking all over for you," Warren exclaimed as he came to stand behind Senai.

Her eyes widened as she turned towards him and she couldn't help but to appreciate the sight in front of her. Warren was sharply dressed in a navy suit with a white shirt underneath that hugged his lean, athletic frame.

"Hey! You look amazing, babe," Senai told him as he took her in for a hug. She could tell he had been drinking because she could smell the scotch on his breath. The fact that he grabbed and squeezed her ample behind even though he was in front of a lot of people was also a telltale sign.

"Come on, baby. I have something to tell you," he said as he basically dragged her towards the stage. Senai started to panic and looked around for help. She caught her grandmother's eyes and knew she had to do this on her own.

Just as he was about to tell the deejay to stop the music, Senai grabbed his hand and pulled him out of the room and into the hallway that led to offices and the bathrooms. She checked the door that she was coming to and seeing as it was unlocked, hurriedly opened it and dragged Warren in behind her before she closed and locked the door.

"Warren," Senai quietly said as she approached him. In the light, she saw a light sheen on his forehead and saw a nervous glint in his eye. "We can't, Ren."

"We can do this, Senai. We're good together."

"We are. We're great together. Doesn't mean we're meant to be together, though."

He sighed heavily before taking a seat on the couch on the other side of the office. Senai walked towards him slowly before taking a seat beside him. He grabbed her hand and squeezed it.

"My mother wants this more than I do," he said, chuckling bitterly and wiped his hand down his face. She knew he loved his parents, but they were the overbearing type, especially his mother.

"I figured. You'll be twenty-six in a few months. That's still so young to make this kind of decision. Especially to someone who you know you don't really wanna marry."

"Hey, you act like I don't love you," he said angrily. She could tell he was getting frustrated but it wasn't with her, moreso the situation.

"Stop it, you know that's not what I mean," she answered gently as she put her hand to his cheek. "I know you love me, Ren. I just know that we aren't supposed to last forever. You know it, too. You're gonna be an amazing surgeon and you need someone who is going to be there every single step of the way, and I'm not that person," she said somberly.

No matter how much she wished she could, she couldn't see herself giving up her career, her life's dream, for him. She couldn't see herself at any point making sacrifices for him that honestly should have been easy for her to make.

Her love for him didn't outweigh her passion. Her love for him wasn't a passion for her at all and it was another reason why she knew they weren't meant to be.

"Yeah, you're right. Just hate to admit it," he said with a deep sigh of defeat. He reached in his coat pocket and pulled out the small, black velvet box and just looked at it before flipping it open. "Deep down, I was hoping you'd say no. Crazy, right?"

"No, I don't think so," Senai said as she cuddled up to him and put her head on his shoulder as she glanced at the beautiful ring in his hand. Beautiful, but not the style she'd want to wear; even more of a sign it wasn't meant to be. "You're going to find you a doting woman who will think the world of you. Someone who will love you just as much as they love themselves. And when you do, you won't have any second thoughts because you'll just know."

He didn't say anything as he put the ring box back into his pocket, but brought his arm around her, moving her head to his chest and kissed her forehead. They sat together silently, soaking in their time together, knowing that it was their last moments of peace before separating forever.

It was bittersweet for Senai. Her *safe*. Her *normal*. Her *routine*. Everything was changing, and after four years, she wanted to have a good cry and smile wide all at once. She was hurting but thankful. Her first heartbreak would be a lesson, but such a blessing. She loved this man, but knew they both needed more.

"Come on, lover boy. It is my party after all," Senai said as she lifted herself from the couch and fixed her dress. He lifted himself up and they both walked to the door. Before she could open it, he stopped her.

"You know if you ever need anything, I'm here, right?" Warren asked as he looked down at her. She stared into his intense brown eyes, remembering every little moment they'd shared over the years. She swallowed the lump in her throat before nodding her head and smiled sadly while trying to hold in her tears.

"Ditto, babe."

21

Chi sat outside of Scottie's home with a smile on his face as he thought about what he was just told. The city was trying to fight them on it, but it looked like they were going to settle for a million dollar settlement for his wrongful imprisonment. It wasn't much in his eyes, basically a teardrop in the middle of the ocean, but it was enough to go in Mercy's college fund.

"Speak," Chi said as he answered his burner phone.

"Looks like you good to go, boss man," Benny said through his car speaker.

"Good looking out, bruh. I'll be heading that way in a few."

"Bet."

Chi stopped at the red light and couldn't help but sigh in contentment. Since his release, things had been working out for him in every way. His wife was happy, his baby girl was spoiled with his presence, and his organization was doing record numbers. Now, all he had to do was tie up loose ends.

Terrance Rhodes had been a thorn in his side for too long and it was time that was rectified. Before he could dig too deeply in his thoughts, he saw he was getting another phone call, this one on his main line.

"To what do I owe the pleasure of you hitting me up today?" Chi answered with a smile.

"Don't act like you don't love when I call. Can you swing by here today if you're free?" she asked.

"You know I got you. I'm actually not far from you. I'll be there in ten."

"Okay. Come right up," she said before hanging up.

He pulled into a park not even eight minutes later and made his way up the elevator. When she opened the door, he smelled food cooking and was glad he decided to come when he did.

"Hope you cooking enough for me, Sen. A nigga is mad hungry," he joked. She playfully rolled her eyes and nodded her head as they both walked into the kitchen.

"Where my sister at?"

"She's with Derrick for the day. They had a morning date and she'll probably be gone 'til tonight."

"Oh, Derrick, huh?" he asked with an attitude. She'd introduced them at Senai's graduation party and he wasn't impressed. He looked like a poser, the type that faked it 'til they made it. That wouldn't be that bad if he wasn't acting like he'd already made it better than everyone else in the room. His baby sister liked the guy though so he'd let him make it. For now.

"Oh, stop it. He's not that bad," Senai giggled looking at his facial expression. She fixed his plate and they went to sit at the dining room table. He looked down at his plate and his eyebrows almost touched his hairline with how surprised he was.

"Since when you cook catfish and spaghetti? I ain't ever seen you put this together," he told her as he tore into his food and damn near moaned. Little Senai could cook almost as well as his own wife and that was saying a lot.

"It's nothing, really. Just something I picked back up not too long ago and thought I'd try it," she said vaguely but Chi just smirked. They may have eaten the meal when their grandmothers cooked, but other than that, it wasn't a go-to. He knew she'd gone to Atlanta a few months back and met up with Siah and his home girl. He'd let her slide about it this time, though.

When they finished their food, Chi with three helpings, they moved to the living room where they sat to watch a movie. He looked over at Senai halfway through the film and saw she was fidgety. He knew her well enough to know that she was nervous about something and knew she didn't invite him over just because she missed him.

"Alright, Sen. Tell me what's up with you," he said after grabbing the remote and hitting the mute button.

"Huh? Oh, umm. It's just—"

"What's going on, Senai? Somebody messin' with you or something?" he asked, sitting up on the couch and facing her completely.

He knew she and her boyfriend had broken up the week before and they seemed amicable, but you never knew with men. Senai didn't bother anyone, but people always tried her and he refused to sit back to let her handle it on her own, even though he knew she more than could.

"No, no, it's nothing like that," she said quickly. She seemed to gather herself before turning to face him. "I heard Mecca talking to you yesterday about going to see Terrance soon."

"Yeah, Ima go visit the nigga today, actually. It's about that time," he said, speaking vaguely but knew she understood. As sweet as she was, she wasn't naive and had been around his family long enough, especially Baby, to be desensitized to that side of their life.

"You need to make him suffer, Chi," she said quietly but with so much venom in her voice that even Chi felt a small chill go down his spine.

"You ain't gotta worry about that, baby girl. I promise I got that motherfucka—"

"He raped her!" she blurted out with teary eyes. He looked over at her and saw her lips tremble.

"What you just say?" he asked breathlessly. He had to have heard her wrong. There was no way that Terrance raped anyone and he knew damned well she wasn't insinuating he raped Moriah. There was just no way.

"It's not my place to say, but I just can't be quiet about it anymore. He hurt her so bad, Chi. It took her so long to be happy again after it happened. She still can't even stay by herself at night," Senai said as her body shook with tears streaming down her face.

"Senai—"

"Malachi," she whispered and he knew she was serious. The only person she called by their real name was Baby, even in a serious situation. "I'm not a killer, but I have imagined myself taking his life more than I care to admit. I know you plan to take him out. But I just...I need you to promise me that you'll make his last minutes hell on earth. *Please* promise me that."

He pulled her to his lap and let her cry it out. He had a feeling that she only cried when she was alone. She probably tried to stay strong for Moriah and being strong for so long with no outlet wasn't healthy.

Just thinking about what his sister must have gone through made him tighten his arms around Senai as his own eyes watered. He wasn't there for her then, but he'd make it better. He'd make sure of it.

"I got you, Sen. I promise he'll understand when I'm done with him," he whispered in her ear as a tear fell from his eye. *He'd make sure of it.*

He was waiting for Terrance to come out for visitation and couldn't help but clench his jaw at the thought of him. He stayed with Senai another hour after she told him about what happened, everything she knew at least, and came straight to the prison where he was being held.

Benny and Ryan met him there and all three went straight to the warden to have a conversation. Baby wanted to come along but had some situations to handle with their gun supply in St. Louis and Chi couldn't wait, especially not after what Senai let him know.

They needed a few minutes alone with Terrance before anything went down, and because the warden owed Mordecai a few favors, it didn't take much to get their time.

"The fuck y'all niggas doin' here?" Terrance croaked out after he was escorted into the room. Chi looked over at him in disgust as he took him in. Terrance had tattoos all over his body, including his face, and they definitely weren't professionally done. His dark skin that once was smooth and vibrant was now ashy and covered with blemishes. Mordecai let him know of his drug problem and it seemed like he was still dabbling in something on the inside.

"You know why I'm here, lil nigga. Time to pay the piper," Chi announced before getting up from his seat and punching him in the face. Terrance fell to the floor hard but laughed as he wiped the blood from his mouth.

"Guess you found out it was lil ole me that got you knocked, huh? Oh well," Terrance laughed before spitting more blood from his mouth.

Before he could continue his taunting, Chi hit him again. And again. And again. He hit him so many times that his lieutenants had to pull him off of Terrance who was in a fetal position on the cement floor.

"You always been a lil pussy nigga. Never woulda thought you was the type to take shit that don't belong to you," Chi said once he calmed down. Terrance wheezed out a laugh before he answered him.

"Ha! You know 'bout that, too? It was worth it. Hearing her lil crybaby ass cry out knowing it wasn't shit she could do. Hell, it belonged to me that night," he hissed with a menacing snicker. Chi tried to attack him again but was held back.

"It's cool. You won't be talkin' all that shit soon. Trust," Chi gritted out.

"That's aight. Just to know I put yo yellow ass behind bars and made lil princess cry is enough for me," Terrance said, as he wobbled to a standing position.

"Get this nigga outta my sight before I put one in him," Chi said as he turned around and shut his eyes. He wanted to shoot Terrance between the eyes, but he had other plans for him and couldn't get ahead of himself.

"You might be done wit' me, but you better watch yo back! Ivy still got a eye on you, nigga!" Terrance slurred out as he was carried from the room.

Chi rode home in complete silence. He was pissed. He wanted to hurt Terrance more than he had but knew he had to be patient. He didn't like how smug he sounded about the Ivy woman. He'd been searching for her for years and never came up with anything. He had a feeling, one way or another, she'd eventually show her face. He'd be ready whenever that was.

Just as he was turning into his driveway, he got a confirmation text on his burner. He smirked as he thought back on what he'd told some of the inmates on the inside to do.

"What you need me to do, bruh? You know I got you," a class-mate of Chi's spoke. He'd been on the inside since he hit nineteen and Chi always made sure he was good so he had his loyalty forever.

"I need that taken care of."

"Oh, hell yeah. I got that for sure."

"Smooth, I need the special."

"Oh, shit. You serious?"

"He hurt my sister, Smooth," Chi said. When he looked at Smooth, he saw a dark look come across his face. He was serving thirty years for killing his stepfather and making his mother a vegetable after finding out they were molesting his then twelve-year-old sister. Chi knew he could get Smooth to handle it and make it a personal mission to make him suffer.

"Say no more. I got you, bruh."

"Bet."

Even though Terrance had been hit a few times by Chi, Smooth and his boys beat him more. When he was barely conscious, they sodomized him with a sharpened wooden chair leg until he passed out. By the time he was found by the guards, he'd succumbed to his injuries and was alone when he died, and most likely in a copious amount of pain, just the way Chi wanted him to be.

He may not have been able to be there for his sister, but he avenged her and felt at peace about it and knew when he gave the news to Moriah, she would be, too.

22

SIAH

"You sure you don't remember your mom telling you anything?" LaShea asked as she sat up in her seat to talk to Siah.

"No, Shea. She just said I should bring you," Siah said with his eyes closed. They were taking an early flight to Chicago and he was still extremely tired from his, Avery, and Bryce's early morning workout he got in before he left Atlanta.

"I know, I know, but it's just weird. I've never been to Chicago with you before. You think it's something bad?" she asked hesitantly. He knew she was an over thinker and would probably worry him the entire flight.

"Av, get your girl," Siah told Avery, who'd come along to be with LaShea. He heard LaShea smack her lips in frustration but did end up sitting back.

"Thanks for letting me come, baby. You know I only saw your parents a few times so this is a big deal," Sharell said close to his ear before she kissed his cheek.

He honestly didn't have any plans to bring Sharell on the trip, but she had the most pitiful look on her face when he told her that his mother wanted LaShea to come, but didn't mention anything about her. He was an asshole but he wasn't a dick so he asked Renee if he could bring her along and although begrudgingly, she told him it was fine.

"Sure thing, Rell. Just enjoy yourself and get to know my peoples," he told her with his eyes still shut.

"I definitely plan to."

When they landed, Siah called his father to let him know they'd made it. Micah wanted to personally come and get him but he fought him on it and let him know that he was riding with Avery who planned on getting a rental.

The ride to Hyde Park was mostly silent with only the radio softly playing for background noise. It was a little after seven in the morning and the Chicago streets were filled with the busy bustle of early work traffic.

They pulled into his parents' driveway and he hopped out of the Mercedes SUV that was a replica of what Avery had back home and went to the trunk to get their bags. Before he could reach in to get his duffle, he felt arms circle his waist and he couldn't stop the smile on his face.

"I missed you," he heard her muffled voice say.

"I just talked to you last night, woman," he said and turned around to hug his mother to him after getting the luggage.

"You know it's not the same. Now, who do we have here?" she asked with a smile.

The girls looked nervous while Avery looked on in awe. He'd met Renee before, but she wasn't dressed as casually and didn't have her body on display like she did in the Nike tights and fitted tee she wore right then. Siah knew Renee looked good for her age so he didn't think much of his friends ogling his mother.

"Ma, you remember my teammate Avery, my girlfriend Sharell, and you know Shea," Siah said to her.

She went straight to LaShea and hugged her tight before whispering in her ear. LaShea giggled and nodded in response. She hugged Avery and Sharell and told everyone to come in for breakfast.

"My husband and youngest son are on their way here so we can eat soon. Make yourselves comfortable until then," Renee said with a smile when they all got into the house before going back to the kitchen.

"Nigga," Avery said as he walked over to Siah. Siah already had an idea what the clown was about to say so he just rolled his eyes.

"I knew yo mama was fine, but damn! You ain't tell me she was *fine*," Avery said with emphasis on the second fine. Siah chuckled at his foolery.

"Nigga, I know my mama is attractive. The fuck you want me to do about it, brag? Besides, you better get all your looks in now before my daddy get here. He don't play that shit."

"Yeah, yeah. Yo daddy scary as shit. Ion need those problems in my life," Avery said looking around before walking back over to LaShea. Siah huffed out a laugh before he answered his ringing phone.

"Aye, tell Mommy that Nai is with me so she has to make enough for her, too," Baby said before Siah could even say hello. His heart skipped a beat when he heard Senai's name, but agreed to his request before going to tell his mother the news.

"You good?" Siah asked Sharell quietly when he made it back to the living room. She nodded, but he could tell something was wrong. He grabbed her chin and turned her head to him so he could look at her, but she couldn't keep his eyes.

"Your mom. She hasn't really said much to me," she said with a shrug.

"She hasn't really said much to anybody, not even me."

"Yeah, but she had a whole private conversation with her," she said as she used her chin to point at LaShea.

"Don't do that, Rell. They know each other more than you two do. Of course she'd talk to her," he told her, trying to keep his attitude in check. He hated when she got entitled. At the same time, he could see her side and tried to be understanding.

"I guess so. I just wish she would talk to me that way. I will be in the family sooner or later so we should start a relationship now. Don't you think so?" she asked.

Siah couldn't help but narrow his eyes in response. They hadn't been together long, not even six months, and she was already thinking wedding bells. He'd have to remember to talk to her about that at another time.

"Well, if you wanna talk to her so bad, then do it. You're more than welcome to go in there," Siah said as he heard the door open in the kitchen followed by Micah's and Baby's voices.

"I think I'll wait until later," she responded as Micah and Baby sauntered towards them. Siah knew how intimidating his father could look so he hugged Sharell to him to make her feel more comfortable.

"Where y'all been?" Siah asked.

"Minding our business," Micah told him as leaned over and gave his son a forehead kiss before looking over at Sharell who looked at him wide eyed. "Hello, young lady. How you this morning?"

"I'm well, sir. Nice to see you again," Sharell responded with her husky voice slightly trembling. While they talked, Siah looked over at his brother and saw him motioning towards the kitchen. He looked back at Sharell and his dad and followed behind Baby.

When he walked into the kitchen, he saw his mother doubled over in laughter and Senai standing beside her with her head thrown back with tears pouring from her eyes.

"What we miss?" Baby asked as he bumped Senai out of the way so he could stand beside Renee.

"Nai Nai was just telling me about how your daddy punked you in the car on the way over," Renee answered before she looked at Senai and started laughing all over again. Baby kissed his teeth and rolled his eyes as he gave a look of contempt to Senai who gave him an innocent, closed-mouthed smile in return.

"What's up, Naiya?" Siah asked as he quickly looked her over. She wore black tights similar to his mother's, with a white cropped tank that showed off her little pudge at the bottom of her abdomen that she'd never been able to get rid of no matter how long she stayed in the gym.

He noticed she had her belly button piercing in and had to hurry and look away before his mind wandered to a dangerous space. Surprisingly, she wore her hair down instead of her signature high ponytail she loved so much and he thought it made her look more mature and even more beautiful.

"Hey, Messi. Your dad and Mecca picked me up right from the gym. Hope I'm not intruding on your visit," she told him in that soft voice he loved so much. Before he could let her know she could never intrude on anything he had going on, he heard a husky voice tinged with jealousy speak instead.

"Messy? That's your nickname?" Sharell butted in with a snort. A snort that made Siah's nose flare in agitation.

People always joke when they hear what Senai called him, but he found it intimately special and he refused for her to feel embarrassed about it. Before he could speak on it, though, Senai's light voice answered in a calm tone that had him subtly adjusting himself in his joggers.

"It's *my* nickname for him. Spelled with an -i, not a -y. You won't have to worry about hearing it much since I'm the only one allowed to call him that. I'm Senai by the way. It's nice to finally meet you," she said with her hand held out to shake. Sharell looked flustered, but put a fake smile on her face and shook her hand.

Siah loved when Senai asserted herself without getting out of character. He looked back over to Senai and gave her a wink before walking towards his girlfriend. If he had looked longer, he would have seen Senai's skin redden with a blush that went all the way to her neck.

They all went to the dining room and had a hearty breakfast while Siah's Atlanta crew got to know everyone better. Micah spoke of a meeting that would happen later that day, one that was extremely important.

Siah looked at Baby, but he too looked confused. He didn't know about a meeting happening and he'd just spoken with Chi the night before and he didn't mention one either. He was curious and a tad bit anxious.

As he was walking from the bathroom after breakfast, Siah saw Sharell and Senai speaking in the living room, right in front of all the family photos. He didn't like it, but Senai didn't look uncomfortable so it appeared nothing was wrong. When he saw her give Sharell a tight smile, he figured everything was cool. At least, he hoped so.

23

———

"Let me holla at you for a second, Messiah," Micah said just as Siah was about to walk into the room. He circled back around and went towards his dad. He saw a serious expression on his face and knew something was up.

"What's goin' on, Pops?"

"I need you to be the calm one in there. I need you to have it together and keep it together," Micah told him with a hand on Siah's shoulder.

"Daddy, you making me anxious. What's up?" Siah said as he looked up at Micah. Micah was usually a serious man but never to the point where he told Siah to be the calm one in a situation. Siah knew the family meeting had to be important, but the fact that he didn't know the point of it was getting to him.

"Just listen to me, alright?" Micah asked. Siah looked at the man whose face and build he'd basically replicated and gave him a nod before walking into the room.

Mordecai, Micah, Renee, Emma, and Isaiah sat closer to the front of the office space while Siah, Baby, Chi, Kiara,

Moriah, and Senai sat closer to the door. Senai wondered why she was called to a family meeting, but Baby and Moriah wouldn't hear otherwise. When everyone was settled, Micah gave Mordecai a nod to start so he walked to the front of the room and turned to his family.

"Thank y'all for showing up on such late notice," Mordecai started.

"Why we here, Pops? We coulda met up at the house or something," Chi called out with his arm around Kiara. Mordecai called him early that morning saying they were having a meeting that he and his wife had to come to. He was on edge since he didn't know what it was concerning and because Kiara was needed. It was rare that the ladies ever came along.

"I needed to speak with everyone and I figured I might as well do it all at once," Mordecai breathed out. He made eye contact with Renee who gave him a smile of encouragement and he continued.

"I lost my wife almost twenty-three years ago. Before she passed, Ronnie wanted to make sure I was going to be okay when she was gone so she took it upon herself to find me...a companion."

"So my mom set you up with someone else?" Moriah asked hesitantly. She didn't remember much of her mother since she died when she was only a toddler, but from what she was told about Veronica Jackson, setting her husband up with another woman seemed a little far fetched. Then again, death could bring about changes.

"Exactly. So I met and befriended a woman who I eventually fell for. Then, Ronnie's cancer took her away and I decided it was best that I focus on only being with the two of you," Mordecai said with a smile, pointing to Chi and Moriah.

Chi took in steady breaths as Kiara rubbed his thigh. He missed his mother and wished he'd had her longer. He also knew, the older he got, that Mordecai was lonely. He never would have thought his father had a woman and let her go. The thought of Mordecai sacrificing his happiness for Moriah and him caused a pang of guilt to go through his chest.

Siah looked around making sure everything was okay. He had a feeling that his uncle was about to drop a bomb and wasn't sure what to expect from everyone else. Seeing how calm his parents and grandparents were, they most likely already knew what was going on so that left his cousins, his sibling, and Senai.

He knew Senai could probably keep Moriah grounded and even Baby to a certain degree, but it was Chi who was a wild card. Even with Kiara there, he was almost as bad as Siah when triggered so he'd have to be ready if something popped off.

Mordecai went through the story of how he searched high and low for years to find his mystery woman, but could never locate her, thanks to Emma. Moriah thought it was sweet how he cared about the woman so much even though he let her go to begin with. The only thing that was bothering her was why he was telling them about this woman to begin with.

"I was finally able to catch up with her after all these years and we've rekindled our relationship," Mordecai continued. Mordecai stood there looking around the office taking in everyone's facial expression. Moriah, Kiara, and Senai looked surprised but happy. Chi and Baby looked shocked while Siah wore a calm but thoughtful look.

Siah was happy for his uncle, but knew his news was the calm before the storm. He saw his uncle give his dad a head nod and he got up from his seat and went outside. He guessed this was the time where he'd need to keep cool and collected. Siah looked over to his mother and saw her fidget in her seat. He narrowed his eyes in suspicion. Something crazy was about to happen, he could just feel it.

"Upon rekindling our relationship, I found out some information that changed my life—that will change our lives—"

"Oh my god. You're not dying are you? You told me you weren't dying," Moriah blurted out. Senai grabbed her hand and squeezed it so her friend could calm down. Senai knew Moriah's thoughts could turn dark with the quickness and no one needed that.

"What? No. I, uh," Mordecai stammered as he rubbed one of his hands down his salt and pepper waves and through his beard. Telling them would be harder than he thought. "We have two children. Together."

Chi felt his chest tighten as he tried to comprehend what his father said. He distantly felt Kiara squeeze his leg but he could barely feel it. Blood rushed through his ears and his hearing faded in and out.

Moriah was two seats over and was going through something similar. Her light skin reddened the more it sank in. Her breathing picked up and she didn't know if she wanted to cry or ask more questions but the lump in her throat was leaning more to the former.

As Mordecai continued telling the group about everything that had happened, Siah saw Micah come back out of the corner of his eye, but he wasn't alone. Behind him was a beautiful light skinned woman around his mother's age.

The longer he looked at her the more he realized who it was and he almost broke his neck trying to look at his uncle who already had his eyes on him and simply shook his head before addressing the rest of them.

"Selena Richardson has raised my two youngest all of their lives and I didn't know, but now that I do, I wanted you all to know who they are to me," Mordecai said as he looked behind all of them towards the door.

"Umm, hello," Selena announced as she made her way to the front of the office. "My name is Selena. I'm sure you all have questions and different opinions about me and our crazy situation. Umm, I just want to apologize for staying away so long and I just want you to know I won't be leaving again," she said in a bashfully quiet voice.

No one spoke after she finished. Siah looked around and was leery about what he was seeing. Chi looked like he was two seconds from shooting her and Moriah was busy holding in tears. Baby was surprisingly quiet but had an unhappy expression on his face.

Before anyone could speak, the door opened again and Malik and LaShea walked in. There was nothing but gasps that filled the room as everyone took them in. Malik, seemingly cool even with tension in the air, walked in cockily and smiled his dimpled grin, before going to Mordecai and hugging him tightly. Mordecai hugged him back, but never took his eyes off of his youngest daughter.

LaShea looked around the room and Siah could tell his friend, now cousin, was freaking out. He hurriedly stood before Selena could make a move and took her hand and led her to Mordecai.

"Shea, this is your dad, Mordecai. Unc, this is LaShea," Siah said as he nudged her to him.

Chi looked at his siblings and couldn't help the tear from falling from his eye as his nose flared. His brother looked just like a younger version of him, a tad darker in complexion, but basically a carbon copy. LaShea resembled Moriah as well and it made his temper flare even more. How his dad decided to be with a woman that kept his children away for so long was beyond him.

Siah looked on as LaShea hugged Mordecai tightly as she cried. She always told him about not knowing her dad, but he never would have put it together that they were related. The thought did pass his mind when Senai saw the family resemblance months before, but he thought it was just a coincidence. Clearly, it definitely was not.

Senai pulled a shaking Moriah to her family to see them. When she saw LaShea all those months ago, she never would have guessed this would have happened. She looked over at Baby and decided to see how he was taking everything.

"Hey," she said quietly as she sat beside him.

"What the fuck, Nai? A whole new set of cousins? This shit is crazy," Baby said as he shook his head.

"It is a little unorthodox, but it's family. You already knew Shea so it's not totally new."

"Yeah, but damn. We gone need some family counseling or something," Baby joked and Senai couldn't help but laugh as she put her head on his shoulder. She knew it would take some time for things to settle for everyone, but she had a feeling everything would work out.

Siah looked around the room and everyone was congregating even if it was a little awkward. That is, everyone but Chi. He saw his older cousin was in the corner with Kiara and he didn't look like he'd calmed at all.

"...nah 'cause this some bullshit, Ari. I can't just act like shit straight," Chi said angrily.

"Aye, boy. You good?" Siah asked as he walked up to

them. He heard the last bit of what Chi said, but needed to see where his head was up close.

"Nah, I ain't good, nigga. Acting like we a big ole happy family and shit."

"Nigga, we are. We tight as hell and they're your siblings. You know I've known Shea for years. She's solid, man."

"So, did you know? Shit, y'all close and everything I find it hard to believe you didn't."

"The fuck you tryna say? Nah, I didn't know but I know now and the shit is cool."

"Yeah, whatever. Then, he wanna be with the damn woman. This bit—"

"Hey! I will allow your feelings to be expressed. But do not run out," Kiara said with a mean mug on her face. None of the women in the family liked hearing a woman being called out of their name unless she actually deserved it and even if Selena seemed a little selfish for this, that didn't make her a bitch.

"Whatever, man. Too much shit for me. I'll holla at you later," Chi said before dapping Siah up and dragging Kiara outside.

"Chi left, huh?" Renee asked as she stepped beside Siah who was still watching the door that Chi and Kiara left out of minutes before.

"Yeah, couldn't handle everything right now."

"I know it's a little overwhelming, but I wish he would have stayed," she responded with a sigh.

"Him leaving might be for the best, Ma. You know when he gets upset he can get crazy. I didn't feel like fighting today."

"Yeah, I guess you're right. How are you handling it?"

"I don't even know. One of my best friends is my first cousin and she has a twin who's responsible for getting his older brother who he's never met outta jail. I mean, you can't make this up," he said with a bemused chuckle.

They turned from the door and looked towards their family. LaShea was under Mordecai, who was holding hands with Selena, but she was talking and laughing with Moriah and Senai while Malik was in deep conversation with Baby and Micah. Isaiah and Emma sat to the side and watched everyone's interactions with proud smiles on their faces.

"Damn," Siah muttered as he put his arm around Renee and walked towards his family, both old and new.

24

SENAI

"Hello," Senai heard as she looked at the Jackson family photos on the wall for the umpteenth time. She turned, caught off guard by someone being so close to her and saw Siah's girlfriend.

She hated to admit it, but she really was beautiful. Where Senai was more pear shaped, being bottom heavy with lots of butt, thighs, and hips, Sharell was more of a Coke bottle and had breasts to match her plentiful thighs and backside.

She didn't want to, but Senai couldn't help but feel a little insecure. She always wished she had more than her handful of breasts and seeing the woman who had the man she wished she could be with having much, much more didn't exactly help.

"Hi," Senai answered with a tentative smile. She didn't think Sharell liked her that much, but she was always a 'kill 'em with kindness' kind of girl so she let it go.

"Could I maybe speak with you for a second?" Sharell asked with her husky voice. Senai loved it. It sounded like a mixture of when you were just waking up in the morning and losing your voice because of a cold. Or a sexy bed voice, but Senai didn't want to think about that.

"Sure. What's up?"

"Stay away from my man," Sharell said with an edge to her voice. The nice tone she had when she came over was gone and was replaced with a territorial and possibly jealous one.

"I'm sorry?"

"You heard me the first time, little girl. I know how you feel about Messiah and I don't blame you 'cause he's definitely worth it. But he's mine so you need to keep away if you know what's good for you."

"You've been with him three seconds and already scared of losing him? Tsk tsk. Gotta work on that," Senai nonchalantly teased. She knew she was getting to Sharell because her thick lips pursed together and her eyes narrowed. Before Sharell could respond, she continued.

"I don't know you that well and I'm sure you don't know much about me. Seeing as I've been around him damn near all of my life though, I do know that if it came down to me or you, I know who he'd choose. With that being said, I'm not going anywhere, but I'm in no position to try to get in your way either."

"That's good to hear. You're beautiful, don't get me wrong. But you're a baby. You haven't lived life and you seem inexperienced. You don't have yourself together in the slightest. You have a room-mate for God's sake. You honestly have nothing that can add to that man's life and a man like that? He needs additives, not take-aways," Sharell answered with a smirk.

Senai was hurt, but refused to show it on her face, so instead, she gave her a smile that didn't show the unshed tears that would certainly fall when she was alone.

"Like I said, I'm not trying to get in your way."

Senai came from her thoughts when her phone dinged from a text. Instead of looking at it, she looked back down at her lap at the residency acceptance letter she'd received that morning, but had just opened.

Her grandmother came from the bathroom and sat back down in her chair, but noticed the look on Senai's face and turned towards her.

"What's going on with you, suga?"

"I got in," she whispered.

"What'd you say?"

"I got in, Grammy," she said at a normal volume as she looked up into her grandmother's face and saw Althea get teary eyed.

"Oh, baby. That's so amazing to hear," Althea said as her voice cracked. "Serenity and Jamaal would be so damn proud of you."

Senai felt her eyes sting from unshed tears as she gave a wobbly smile. "I hope so."

Senai talked to her grandmother for the rest of the afternoon. They called Jonathan who was probably more emotional than Althea. Knowing her family was proud of her made her extraordinarily happy and she was glad she told them first.

IT HAD BEEN a week and a half since Mordecai introduced Selena and his children to the family. It was still tense and a little awkward, but things were calming down. Moriah and LaShea were getting along faster than everyone thought they would and Malik mixed in with the Jackson boys like he'd been with them his entire life.

Chi still hadn't come around. Kiara let everyone know he was taking everything in and he was still processing everything, though he had spoken some with his siblings. He wanted nothing to do with Selena, but she was understanding and knew it would take some time, if at all.

Senai drove back to her apartment with a lot on her mind. She knew she was telling Baby and Moriah the news before the rest of the Jackson family, but didn't know who she wanted to tell first. As she pulled into the parking garage, she knew it would probably be better to tell Moriah first and Baby after since she was more emotional by nature.

Moriah was coming from Mordecai's house since LaShea and Avery's flight was leaving sometime that evening and she wanted to say her goodbyes. Siah and Sharell left days before since Sharell had to get back to work and Malik and Selena were in Chicago to stay.

Just as she was getting comfortable on the couch, Moriah came through their door with a big smile on her face.

"Hey, you," Moriah grinned as she walked to the kitchen to get a bottle of water.

"Hey," Senai said with a smile of her own. Her best friend had been so busy with her family and her boyfriend that they hadn't seen each other as often as they usually do.

Senai had her Pandora radio on the bluetooth speaker and Moriah was being her goofy self and twerking like the little girl from one of her favorite shows, *Bob's Burgers*. Senai couldn't help but have a fit of laughter. The song went off so Senai turned down the music and looked at Moriah who was gulping down her water.

"Riah," she called out.

"What's up, babes?"

"I got my residency acceptance today," Senai said and it must have taken a few seconds for it to register because Moriah stood still before screaming loudly and running over to Senai and lifting her off the couch to hug her tightly.

"Oh my God! This is great fucking news! Ahh! Best news

I've gotten in forever! Which part of Chicago are you going to? Northwestern? No, Kindred, right? I can't beli—"

"I'm going to Boston Children's Hospital, Riah," Senai interrupted softly. The smile slowly slid from Moriah's face and her hazel green eyes got glossy before she lowered herself down on the couch. "Say something, please."

"Boston. I—I didn't even know you were seriously considering anywhere but here," Moriah said softly as she looked up at Senai. Senai chewed on her lip to keep it from quivering. The look Moriah was giving her was almost too much to take.

"It's one of the best pediatric hospitals in the country. I put in for it, but I didn't think much of it. I honestly didn't think they'd choose me."

"Oh, please. Why wouldn't they?" Moriah asked sardonically. She shook her head and closed her eyes tightly before looking back at Senai. "I'm sorry, that wasn't very nice."

"It's okay," Senai asked with a teary smile. She knew Moriah could lash out when she was hurt, but she always apologized right after. Neither girl said a word as Senai sat down beside Moriah and Moriah grabbed her hand.

"You're running," Moriah said after sitting silently for a few minutes.

"Yes," she answered simply before turning towards her best friend. "I've had you and Mecca as my backbone for so long and Warren was always there, too. I've never been alone, Riah, not truly. I graduated high school at sixteen and I just graduated medical school at twenty-three. Not many can say that, but I still feel like I'm lacking somehow. I need to run to something different, somewhere new. I need to find out what grown-up Senai is all about."

"And what if grown-up Senai doesn't wanna be in the Chi anymore?"

"My family is here. My *sister* is here," Senai said as she poked Moriah in one of her dimples. "I'll be back."

"We've never been separated, Nai. Damn near twenty years and we've never been apart."

"You'll visit when you can and so will I. Only about a three hour flight," Senai said and Moriah nodded slowly.

"I'm proud of you, Senai Janell Williamson. So, so proud."

"Thank you. I love you, Moriah Vanora Jackson."

"I know," Moriah said smugly as they both laughed quietly and Moriah wiped the tears from her face with the back of her hands.

"When I do come back," Senai started and Moriah made a noise to show she was listening even though her head was down. "I'll be getting my man once and for all."

Moriah snapped her neck so fast to look over at her, she almost laughed but she was serious and confident in her proclamation, so instead, tilted her head and raised her eyebrows daring Moriah to think she was kidding.

"Excuse me?"

To be continued...

Thanks again for taking a chance on this written journey with me! Please join the Jacksons in the last installment of this series, *Off the Wall 3*!

You can reach Ty Ringo at noveltyringo@gmail.com.